# SLOW KISS
# OF THE
# APOCALYPSE

By Keith Kareem Williams

ISBN: 154673483X
ISBN-13: 978-1546734833

apoc·a·lypse  (n) : a great disaster : a sudden and very bad event that causes much fear, loss, or destruction

## PROLOGUE

# MISSING

Only a parent would, or ever truly could, completely understand how it feels when one of their children was even an hour late to get home. The fear and concern would always be there, even long after their child were grown. A billion ugly, awful scenarios always ran through a true parent's mind as they watched the digits on the digital display flip by or the hands on the clock move as time ticked by, terrified about why they hadn't heard from their beloved *baby*. In fact, mothers and fathers spend so much time fearing for their children's safety that it is no wonder that they go gray and lose their hair so young sometimes. Children were probably responsible for more heart attacks and strokes than poor eating habits and old age. Now, imagine a daughter being gone for two whole days and how much panic that would cause in a loving mother's heart and mind.

"Where did you say your daughter works again?" Police Officer Heath Crosby asked as he continued to scribble down pertinent information in his little black notebook, in his sloppy, fifth grade handwriting.

"I already told you that three times already officer. Why do you keep asking me that?" Claire Hughes asked Crosby, frustrated that he seemed to have stopped really paying attention to what she was trying to tell him a good five minutes ago.

"Well, it's just that..." Crosby started to answer.

"It's just that *what?*" Claire asked, annoyed by the smirk on Crosby's face and his seeming lack of regard for the fear she felt in her heart.

Claire Hughes had been to the precinct the day before and they sent her home after telling her that her daughter wouldn't be considered a missing person until more time had passed. So, she politely complied despite her intuition screaming that something terrible must have happened. Now that she was back again, trying to get the police to help her find her daughter who uncharacteristically hadn't come home or even called in two days, she found that they weren't being very helpful.

"Well, you see, it's just that the club where your daughter works doesn't have the best reputation. The girls that work there..." he started to say but Claire cut him off again.

"The reputation of the girls who work there doesn't have anything to do with my daughter being missing for two days. My daughter isn't like some of the other girls that work there," Claire snapped back while pointing an angry finger at officer Crosby.

"Awww c'mon lady," he chuckled sarcastically and leaned back in his chair. He dropped his cheap Bic pen on the desk and flipped his little black notebook shut. "So, you're telling me that YOUR daughter just happens to be the ONLY *good girl* that works down at that club? Because let me tell you lady…most of the ones I know about are loose and slutty, to be completely honest with you," he said.

"No you don't. Don't you dare!" Claire yelled, completely tired of the officer's lack of concern for the seriousness of the situation but also because of his not-so-subtle attempt to brand all of the girls that worked at the club as wild, immoral floozies. She wasn't going to let him get away with that.

"Look lady…is it really that hard to believe that your daughter went to work, met some high-roller, deep-pockets, baller-type and ended up leaving the club with him? She's probably asleep, safe and sound in some basketball player's five-star hotel suite," he said.

"No. My daughter wouldn't go two days without calling me to let me know where she was," Claire insisted.

"Ma'am, trust me. This kind of thing happens all the time. But, we'll go down to the club since that's the last place she was supposed to be right?" he asked.

"Yes, that's the last place she called me from," Claire answered as she wrung her hands together from worry and fought desperately to hold in tears.

"Fine," Crosby sighed. "Now go home and get some rest. You look like you haven't slept in a while. We'll call you if we find out anything and you let us know if your daughter contacts you or turns up."

"Okay," Claire agreed wearily as she stood up on tired legs. She clutched her purse close to her chest as she started to leave.

"Don't worry. Young women pull this type of shit

all the time. I have four daughters and I can't tell you how many times they've nearly given me and my wife strokes. Your daughter will turn up eventually with a story and a million excuses for why she didn't come home or call. You'll see," Crosby tried in vain to reassure the distraught mother on her way out of the precinct.

Nothing in this world except for her daughter showing up at home, safe and sound could convince Claire Hughes that something horrific hadn't happened to her child. The ugly world they lived in ate young women alive all the time.

# PART 1
# THE FACE OF DEATH

afely secured behind the locked door of the only private dressing room in Club Xplosive, she sat at the vanity and prepared for what was going to be one of the most important shows of her young career. It had been a very difficult road to get that opportunity because the route she had taken was very different from most of the other pretty girls who wanted to be famous. In her first life, she vaguely remembered showing up to auditions, dolled-up, bright-eyed and full of hope. Back then, she sang from her heart with innocent joy, eager to share her voice with any and all that would listen. She came close to fulfilling her dreams and being discovered once in those days but that road had ended in with an unfortunate, traumatic event that had led to her rebirth. Of course, the term *rebirth* implies that she had died and that is exactly what had happened to her, literally. Everything she had been before her heart had stopped beating had changed her into something else that not even she quite understood as her old soul had floated away like an untethered helium balloon. In her second life, she was able to vividly visualize every action she had taken to get to where she was. This time around, her vocals came from a different part of her soul. Her eyes were finally open wide enough that she recognized and understood the raw truths about the world. She had lost all of her precious innocence in her first life. All that was left after her rebirth was her uncanny acceptance of harsh realities that most people feared to acknowledge.

"I hate my face," she thought while staring at her own reflection in the filthy, dressing room mirror as she applied her mascara.

If anyone had heard her say such a thing out loud, they would have thought her insane for making such a self-hating statement because for most of her life, everyone had always considered her to be quite gorgeous. There weren't many who could rival her natural beauty, with her big, beautiful, dark brown eyes. Men and women alike couldn't help but wonder what it was like to kiss her thick, luscious, pouty lips. When she used make-up to enhance those features she almost had no equal but still, she hated and despised the way she looked. In a world where everyone wanted to be pretty, she knew how odd and out-of-place her self-image was but most people were blind to how much pain her perceived prettiness had brought her. With those seductive eyes, she had seen the look of hatred on the faces of the women who considered themselves not-so-pretty, no matter how humble or nice she tried to be. For absolutely no reason at all, without even knowing her, they despised her just for existing the way God's hand had made her. The venom they often spewed in her direction was cruel and seemed as wicked as the mischief on the serpent's tongue in that first primordial garden. In the faces of those that desired her, she recognized the burning, ravenous lust that tainted her trust because she knew firsthand how dangerous it was. Far too many times she had been undressed by disrespectful, reckless eyes and assaulted by unwelcome, uninvited hands. She supposed that was why she felt so safe when she kept her face hidden behind her ornate masquerade masks.

For her performance that night, she had chosen one of her favorites. The color scheme of the Venetian mask was red and black to match her red dress and black, red-bottomed, high-heeled shoes. The winding, filigreed pattern glittered and she imagined how it would sparkle under the overhead stage lights. Two artificial feathers, one red and one black, were attached to the right side of the mask by an ornate button that resembled a precious piece of jewelry, highlighted by the ruby-colored stone at its center. Once she put it on, it would only cover the top portion of her face, leaving her lips and her beautiful eyes exposed but those were the parts of her that she needed to show so that she could seduce her audience with more than just her voice. Everything was a tool to be used, from the wet look of her lipstick to the deep cleavage of her dress.

"Cali, it's almost show time. Time to hit the stage baby," shouted Seerule Ramzi, the club manager, from the other side of her dressing room door after he had knocked politely.

*Cali*, she thought. It was strange to hear people call her that because that was not what her parents had named her. It was who she had become and the persona she took on every night to the roar of the applause from her rabid fans. At first, it was someone she pretended to be whenever she performed for an audience but eventually, she had evolved to feel more comfortable in that role as opposed to who she was before.

"I'll be right out," she answered in a voice that was feminine but also deep and flowed as smoothly as raw honey.

Cali stood up and took one more look at herself in the mirror as she straightened her short, red dress. It was tight and hugged her curves in all the right places. Although she looked exactly how she wanted to look, she frowned before she reached for her mask and secured it tightly on her face. She turned from the mirror and walked to the dressing room door without having to look at her reflection again because now, she knew exactly who, and what she was.

All of the chatter and friendly banter between the girls that worked as employees of the club was replaced with a muted hush as Cali walked by on her way to the main stage. None of them greeted her and she in turn greeted none of them or even appeared to acknowledge their presence. A few of the exotic dancers, waitresses and VIP section bottle service girls looked on with quiet admiration but the majority of them gave her dirty looks. Cali was solely focused on the task at hand and simply didn't care.

"You know, a simple hello would go a long way with breaking the ice with the ladies around here. I get the vibe that they don't like you very much," Seerule joked.

"I don't want to break the ice. I like it cold. Besides, they don't pay me to perform and they don't buy my music. I keep the place packed and I am the reason they get such good tips," she answered with an arrogant chill in her voice.

"That's fine. It was just a suggestion," Seerule shrugged. He had grown accustomed to her attitude and occasionally odd demands. As a professional, he expected eccentricities from creative, talented folk and chalked it up to the nature of celebrities.

Although she did walk with an air of superiority, Cali's disdain for the girls that worked at the club did not come from a place of pure arrogance, as most would assume. She behaved the way she did because she pitied them and felt great disappointment to a certain degree. Aside from the miniscule minority of girls who actually were working there just to pay for school, the majority of them sought employment at the club in hopes of somehow catching the attention of one of the wealthy patrons that frequented the establishment. In fact, many of them had broken it down to an exact science. They knew the difference between a guy who was spending his income tax refund or his rent money to try to appear as if he was well-off as opposed to the man who really could afford to spend without conscience or detrimental financial consequences. Once they were fortunate enough to get a wealthy man to take notice of them, they did whatever it took to reap the rewards of sharing their bodies with men who would never view them as more than toys to be played with, then discarded. In Cali's opinion, a woman's body was

5

worth more than handbags, designer shoes and a vacation or two. She believed that they sold their souls for cheap and didn't deserve her respect. The occasional "bitch" hissed at her back didn't bother her one bit. She viewed them all as walking ghosts because in her mind, it was only a matter of time before they were left hollow, spent carelessly like loose change, used up and abandoned with only memories of the days when they had been pretty to comfort them in the midst of miserable lives. There was no future in the path they had chosen.

"You ready?" Seerule asked her as they reached the metal door that separated the rear of the club from the stage area.

"Always," she answered confidently.

"Knock 'em dead," he said as he pushed the door and held it open for her.

"Every time," was her response before she stepped out into the spotlights.

## PART 2
# ALL OF THE LIGHTS

After exchanging pleasantries with the live band, Cali strolled onto the stage with the measured, controlled, graceful stride of a supermodel. The stage was her coliseum, her arena and her temple. It was the place where she felt most alive, in all of her mysterious glory, to be worshipped, envied, desired and admired. Whenever she stood underneath the hot beams from all of the overhead lights, she became a goddess with power in her presence and her voice. The band played softly in the background as she stepped to the edge of the stage with seductive sensuality in the way her hips swayed. The exotic dancers stopped dancing and the waitresses stopped serving drinks because, despite how much some of them might have disliked her, she had an irresistible aura that demanded their undivided attention. In fact, the entire club had gone quiet as every person with a pulse stared at her, all of them completely in awe. For a moment, she looked back into the sea of stranger's faces. She blew the crowd a kiss, raised one hand in the air and signaled for the band to begin.

Cali's soulful, sultry vocals combined with the music from the live instruments played by the band held every single person inside of Club Xplosive in a trance. The way she danced in the short, red dress made most of the men and even some of the straight women wonder what she might taste like if only they could explore a little higher up her thighs, just above what her scandalous hemline kept hidden. The mask that concealed so much of her face made them even more curious about her. The glimpse of her lips and her eyes encouraged their wildest imaginations in very much the same manner that the sensual tease had been mastered and employed by the best burlesque dancers. It was human nature to crave the things they couldn't have and to become obsessed with any mystery that proved difficult to uncover or solve.

Twenty minutes and four songs later, Cali the songstress prepared to perform her final tune for the night. Both of the band's guitar players stepped forward out of the dimly lit section of the stage and came under the bright beams of the spotlights. Their stage presence and both of their vocals were an integral part of her finale.

Paul "Strings" Blake took his place to Cali's left. He was tall, dark and exactly the type of handsome that made women toss their panties at the stage when he performed. His voice was raspy, rough and full of the raw emotion that expressed his experiences over the course of a rugged life. He was full of testosterone and overflowed with masculine sexuality. On Cali's right, Justin "Shy" Tie strummed the strings of his guitar with nimble, skilled fingers but kept his eyes to the ground. He was nowhere near the prototypical alpha male that Paul was but he did possess an awkward, nerdy charm. In fact, he was so boyish and meek in demeanor that one almost expected his mom might show up any minute and drag him away for staying out past his curfew or not finishing his chores. There was a brief pause before all three of them began the final song.

As Paul belted out his verse with passionate conviction, Cali pressed her body close to his and danced all over him like one of the strippers. She put her face closer to his as if they were going to kiss as they sang and grooved together. Everything about their performance together was sexually charged, raw and almost animalistic. Then, it was time for young Justin to join in and add his voice to the tune. Cali crossed over to his side of the stage but their chemistry was deliberately different by design. Justin pretended to blush when she put her hand on his shoulder and played up the "shy guy" persona to perfection. Unlike the adult, X-rated duet with Paul Strings, Cali and Justin Tie flirted on stage like inexperienced teenagers for the pleasure of the people in the crowd who enjoyed seeing the geek get the girl. The baby-faced bassist seemed self-conscious and timid on purpose to give the impression that he had very little, or no experience with women. They finished their performance which was immediately followed by thunderous applause as the patrons ate it all up and loved every second of it.

Cali bathed in the sound of a packed house full of clapping hands as she smiled and scanned the venue. Then, she spotted the man she had been looking for, drinking champagne in one of the club's dimly-lit VIP sections. He was surrounded by his friends, associates and a fair amount of sexy, scantily-clad women but his eyes were definitely fixed on Cali in her Venetian mask and tight dress. The look on his face said that he was impressed.

# PART 3

# SECRET ADMIRERS

Cali sat in her dressing room with her arms folded, her legs crossed in her red dress with her mask and make-up both still on her face. She had kicked off her shoes to give her toes and the soles of her feet some relief from the soreness caused by all of the dancing she had done during the show. Few people knew how difficult it was to dance in high heels. She shook her leg impatiently until she heard what she had been waiting for, the gentle rapping on her dressing room door.

"Are you decent? Can I come in?" the male voice asked from the other side of the door.

"Come in," she said, immediately recognizing that it was the owner of the club, Gabriel Frost, who had come calling. She had been expecting him. "It's open."

"Great show tonight," Gabriel told her as he walked into the dressing room and closed the door behind him.

"Thank you. I always try my best to give it my all," she answered.

"Yes, you do. They come from far and wide to see Cali, the tasty temptress, the seductive siren, the gorgeous goddess. We had a packed house thanks to you," he said as he loosened his silk necktie.

"You flatter me but, I'm just a small part of what goes on here. You created this establishment. This is your baby," she humbly thanked him.

"You underestimate your value," the swarthy man told her as he grabbed a swivel chair from the corner of the room, slid it next to her and sat down beside her.

"What's on your mind?" she asked, sensing that he had made a rare appearance in her dressing room with a more pressing purpose than just showering her with flowery compliments.

"Well, no sense in beating around the bush so I'll get right to it then. One of the gentlemen in the VIP section has made a special request," he started to explain.

"Really? And exactly what kind of special request would that be?" she asked, pretending to be surprised although she actually had a good idea who it was who had prompted Gabriel to pay her a visit on his behalf. She remembered how that man looked at her when she had been on stage.

"The man I'm referring to seems to be quite fascinated and enthralled with you so he asked me to arrange a private meeting with you."

"A *private* meeting huh? I'm flattered but no thanks. Send one of the strippers or the bottle service girls, your glorified bar wenches, to see about his needs," she grumbled.

Gabriel skillfully feigned a surprised expression and gestured away her misgivings with a wave of his hand.

"Wait, wait, wait. You don't understand."

"No, you're wrong. I totally OVER-stand what's going on. Some of these men come in here, eagerly buy overpriced liquor, throw money at the dancers and feel like they can just buy anything and believe that everything is for sale. Go back and tell that guy, whoever he is, that I'm not a prostitute and that he can't afford a minute of my time," she told him.

"You didn't give me chance to finish. The man who wants to meet you is a record producer. Ever heard of Chadwick Grossman?" he asked.

"Of course I have. Every musician, band, singer, and rapper knows that name, seen his multi-platinum album credits," Cali answered.

"Well, THAT'S who's asking to meet you. He's a friend of mine from way back so I invited him to watch you perform tonight. He likes what he saw and what he heard. He thinks he can take you, your natural talent and this whole mystery woman gimmick you have going on and transform it into something bigger. He wants to turn you into a diva, a pop star, a worldwide phenomenon if you let him help you. So, go ahead and meet with the man. He's trying to get money with you babe…not trying to fuck you," said Gabriel as he got up to leave.

"Fine. If it really is about business and building my career, I'll meet with your friend," she sighed, still suspicious of Gabriel's friend's true intentions. "Oh, and by the way Gabriel….no matter what they say, even when money really IS the main motive, they ALL still want to fuck, sooner or later," she told him.

"You're something else," he said, shaking his head. "I'll tell Chadwick to have the valet get his car and you can meet him around back. You get yourself together and I'll have Seerule wait with you outside. Do this for me. Chadwick has a lot of influence on social media and with his artists who can endorse me.

His support is important for my campaign. I need this," he told her before he walked out of her dressing room and shut the door behind him.

Gabriel had always been kind to her, never rude or made a single, inappropriate sexual advance so she felt slightly guilty that she had lied to his face. She had known who Chadwick Grossman was all along because she had met him once before, in her first life. Back then, he was nothing that even slightly resembled the music mogul he would eventually become. She had known him when he was just an aspiring record producer who sold cocaine, pills, mushrooms and marijuana to pay for studio time. Secretly, as soon as she had started her second life, she had sought him out but by the time she finally found him, he had become such an iconic giant in the music industry that it was impossible to get anywhere near him. She had finally decided to employ a devious scheme to attract him to HER instead and much to her delight, it seemed to have worked out almost perfectly. She smiled as she slipped on her shoes and waited for Seerule to show up to escort her to the back of the club. Her night had just gone from mediocre and routine to extremely exciting.

"I know this guy is supposed to be the boss's buddy and all but, I've heard stories about him. You sure you don't want me to send one of the security dudes from the front door with you to watch your back, just in case?" Seerule asked Cali while he waited on the lonely block behind the club with her.

"Aww, you're so sweet. Thanks for the offer but I'll be fine," Cali answered, her voice slightly muffled underneath the black scarf that covered the lower half of her face. She had always sensed that Seerule had a crush on her and she found it cute that he was being so protective.

"Okay, but be careful," he told her as Chadwick finally pulled up to the curb at the entrance of the alley where they were standing.

"Don't worry about me. I'm a big girl," Cali said and gave him a friendly hug before she strolled over to the passenger side of the white Phantom, Rolls Royce.

Seerule had a horrible, sinking feeling in his gut as he watched the luxury vehicle speed away. He hadn't had the chance to tell Cali about some of the more disturbing things that he'd heard but, Chadwick Grossman had been rumored to have unhealthy, abnormal sexual appetites that would be frowned upon in even the kinkiest circles. He wasn't quite sure if the sexy singer that he had eyes for even knew what she might have gotten herself into. Over the course of his tenure as club manager, his duties had included tending to the eccentric requests of the celebrities, professional socialites, high-paid athletes, and rich people who frequently patronized the upscale establishment. He often pondered what it was that gave the privileged such odd tastes. One of the conclusions he had come to was that sheer boredom drove them to seek unique thrills and strange sensations. Wealth, stardom and the absence of financial restraints made it possible for them to almost do whatever they wanted which transformed them into deviants and creeps. They were so desensitized to the things that excited normal folk that they developed freaky fetishes and frequently engaged in strange behavior. He spat a wad of phlegm into the gutter before he turned around to head back inside.

"Good evening Miss Cali," Chadwick said as he stared hard at her soft, creamy thighs, barely covered by her short, dress, while the car idled at a red light.

"It's Cali Mr. Grossman," she answered, quickly correcting his mispronunciation by stretching out the "a" in her name to sound like it did in the word "ah" because the way he had said it made it more like the short "a," as in the word apple, almost as if Cali was short for California.

"Cali you say?" he asked, pronouncing it correctly according to her. "Like the Hindu goddess of death?"

"Yes, just like the goddess of death. She is also the goddess of time, change, power and destruction. Her name also means time, or death…as in time has come," she answered cryptically.

"Well, I see you've put a lot of thought into that answer. You spell it with a K too?" he asked in a slightly mocking tone and as the light turned green, he floored the gas pedal.

"No, it's Cali with a C," she answered with her back pressed firmly against the passenger seat because of the speed he was driving. She was glad that she had been wise enough to fasten her seatbelt when she first got in the car with him.

"So, what's the deal with the mask and now this scarf over your face? I was hoping to find out if you're as pretty as I think you are under there," he said as he took a turn so sharply that the car's tires screeched like a banshee.

"That's a personal question. I thought this was a business meeting?"

"This IS a business meeting and that was a business question. Before I decide if I want to invest my time in working with you or not, I need to know certain things…like if there's some kind of deformity that you're trying to hide. I'd kinda like to know that sorta thing before I decide to parade you around in front of the world," he told her.

"You've already decided that you're going to work with me. Otherwise, I wouldn't be here in this car with you," she said.

"Oh? You think so? Don't be so sure sweetheart. Until I give you a contract to sign, you're still on probation with me and nothing, absolutely NOTHING at all is guaranteed."

Cali wondered how many girls he must have run the same game on. She wondered how many times he had tried to exploit another person's dreams and how many of those ambitious dreamers ended up getting played in the worst kind of way.

"And where are we going exactly anyway?" she asked, looking out of the tinted passenger side window at nothing but a blur of unfamiliar streets.

"Just relax and enjoy the ride. You'll see when we get there," he answered.

# PART 4
# SKULL & BONES

The pulsating jets of hot water from the showerhead in Chadwick's shower felt heavenly against Cali's naked skin as she washed away the sensation of his groping, unwelcomed touch. It was like rain with a rhythm as it beat down on her, soothing and relaxing her. She was almost jealous that she didn't have one just like it in her own tiny apartment. Once she had washed all of the soap from her body, she stepped out of the shower, careful not to trip over Chadwick who was tied up on the bathroom floor.

"I hope you don't mind that I used your shower. It's really, really nice. I couldn't resist," Cali said to him as she grabbed one of his clean white towels from the rack on the wall.

Chadwick squirmed around on his belly with his hands and feet bound with thick, black, plastic zip ties. He tried to mumble some sort of plea or protest that she couldn't understand because she had stuffed her black, lace panties in his mouth as a make-shift gag to ensure that he couldn't yell for help. She didn't need anyone coming to his rescue and ruining the intimate evening that she had meticulously planned for some time.

"I bet you didn't see this coming," she said to him while she dried her hair in front of the bathroom mirror.

Because of his restraints, he couldn't answer her of course but he definitely had not expected to end up hogtied in his own apartment. Just as he had done with countless wanna-be starlets and vixens, he had lured her back to his upscale penthouse to make promises he never intended to keep so that he could enjoy her sexually in every way imaginable. When they first arrived at his place, everything had been going well according to his plan. However, Cali had proved to be harder to get than he had anticipated but he was fine with that. In fact, it excited and aroused him that she had put up such a strong resistance to his advances. When he finally got her to reveal her face, he was certain that he was closer to having her in his king-sized bed with her legs spread. When he realized that she was determined not to sleep with him, he decided that another tactic was necessary so he tried to ply her with alcohol laced with a narcotic pill that always did the trick. Every woman that took that drug, knowingly or unwittingly, always gave up the sex eventually. Like a hungry wolf, he licked his lips and watched as she took her first sip. He remembered taking one right after from his own glass but that's when everything went fuzzy, right before he must have blacked out. When he finally opened his eyes again, he was bound and gagged on his own bathroom floor. He figured that she must have drugged him then dragged him in there while he was unconscious but for what purpose, he had no clue. He prayed that it was just some sort of freaky sex play.

"You know, this turned out to be much easier than I thought it was going to be. When I showed you my face, I was worried that you might recognize me right away. That would have been awkward if you had and it would have definitely complicated things. We met once before you know…in my first life," she told him.

Cali stepped around him carefully, went over to the bathtub and turned on the faucet. She sighed, sat on the edge of the porcelain tub and waited for it to fill up with water. She used the heel of her bare foot to roll Chadwick over to make sure that he would be facing her before she spoke again.

"I have to admit that I felt some kind of way when you didn't recognize me but I guess since our first violently intimate meeting, there must have been hundreds of other girls with stardust and glitter in their eyes, hoping for fame, especially with you being such a big shot now and all. But, I wonder how many of them ended up like I did? How many of them ended up left for dead in that filthy, polluted river?"

She watched Chadwick squint, straining his eyes to see her clearly as he desperately searched the vaults of his memory. Cali smiled when those baby-blue eyes opened wide when he finally recognized her.

"I can tell by the look on your face that you probably remember me now. And if you do, then I think you know that this night is not going to end well for you…just like that night at the end of my first life didn't end well for me," she said to him. "It's really funny how those old bones never truly stay buried forever isn't it?"

Chadwick began to thrash about on the floor like a floundering fish on the deck of a boat. Cali ignored his muffled pleas for mercy as she watched the water level rise slowly in the bathtub. Once it was full, she shut off the faucet and turned her attention back to her captive.

"I'm pretty sure that right about now, you probably want to beg me not to do whatever it is I'm about to do to you. Of course, I'm only guessing because I can't understand a word you're saying with my panties still stuffed in your mouth but remember…YOU were the one who said you wanted to see what I taste like," she reminded him sarcastically. "Well, time to do what I really came here to do all along," she said as she stood up.

Cali walked over to Chadwick, leaned down close to his face and kissed him sweetly on the cheek. Then she roughly grabbed a handful of his golden blonde hair and dragged him over to the edge of the bathtub. He struggled and made it difficult for her to move him until she kicked him in the gut and then stomped hard on his private parts which briefly put a stop to all of his resistance. With great effort, she hauled him over the edge of the tub as he groaned in agony. As soon as he realized what was happening, he started to struggle again, desperate and hoping beyond hope that he might find a way to break free. She had all the leverage as she pushed his face beneath the surface of the water with her full weight pressed down on his back as she straddled him.

Killing a person in real life isn't anything like what they show in the movies. As brutal and as gruesome as it seems on the big screen, it's actually even worse in reality. When a human being senses that their imminent demise is at hand, even the weakest person fights back with a ferocity that rivals any creature in the animal kingdom. Despite Chadwick being bound, it took all of her strength to hold him down. She gritted her teeth as her arms strained to keep his head submersed under the bath water. Finally, just before her muscles gave out, the air bubbles from his nose stopped breaking the surface and Chadwick Grossman finally stopped moving. When she was certain that he was drowned, she turned his body over so that he floated face up. She looked down into his empty, lifeless eyes and smiled, satisfied that he had finally paid for his heinous crime against her when she was a different person, in a different time. She forced her hand between his clenched teeth and dragged her panties out of his mouth.

## PART 5
# THE VOYEUR

While Chadwick Grossman's corpse floated in the bathtub, Cali casually got dressed in the main living area of the posh loft. A great weight had been lifted from her shoulders and she felt slightly at peace because of what she had just done. She would have been even more content if she didn't have much more work to do. Still, it was a great start and there was at least one major name that she could cross off of her "death list," as she called it. She was so lost in her own thoughts that she hadn't noticed that someone out on the balcony watched her every move with great interest but mysterious intentions.

The quiet voyeur had witnessed everything that had transpired that night but he hadn't made a move to intervene or make his presence known. Even Chadwick hadn't known that the stranger was there. The heavyset man with the beer belly sat on a deck chair smoking a cigar and sipping expensive champagne as he enjoyed the live drama that had unfolded in front of him. Although he had hoped to see them have sex, what came next was almost as good. He was slightly aroused by the way Cali flawlessly executed her plot for revenge that night. She turned out to be devious, deliberate, crafty and cunning, all things that he admired in a woman. He enjoyed watching her put her clothes back on just as much as when she had stripped out of them after drugging Chadwick.

Once she was fully dressed again, Cali composed herself and calmly walked through the front door of the loft as if nothing had happened. After she was gone, the mysterious observer stood up and buttoned the front of his grey suit jacket after he sucked in his gut. For a man of his massive girth, it was almost a cruel joke that he was sometimes known as Famine. Only a few knew his true nature and even they rarely dared to address him as such. He preferred to be called Herman, the name his mother had given him in a life that he had lived before. That past where he had been a normal, mortal boy was many lifetimes ago but he had never fully managed to free himself from the echoes of it. Whenever he looked at himself in the mirror, he certainly thought he looked a lot more like a "Herman" than that other thing he had become.

Herman sent a thick, white cloud of cigar smoke into the night air and walked over to the edge of the balcony. His stomach roared like a lion as he peered over the side of the building, down twenty stories to the street below. No matter how much he ate, his constant, insatiable hunger was the most unpleasant aspect of his curse. His only relief came when he was able to transfer that starving feeling to others, which he did, as often as he could. That evening, it had been his turn to keep a close watch on Cali but all he could think of in that moment was how soon he would be free to feed after he was relieved from his assignment. He took his cell-phone out of his pocket when she finally appeared, as tiny as an ant, hundreds of feet on the street below. He watched her walk out of the front entrance of the building, flag down a yellow taxi and hop in. As soon as the cab drove off, Herman ran his hand against the smooth skin on his scalp. He was as bald as a bowling ball but once upon a time, he had a wild head full of red hair which used to grow way too fast according to his mother who would give him haircuts in their kitchen. Now, it didn't grow at all, at least not on the top of his head. He had a bushy red hipster beard and hair seemed to spring wildly from other places on his body where he wished it would not. He dialed one of his only two friends in the world and waited for him to answer.

Just before he stepped into the elevator, Yusef saw Herman's number pop up on the incoming call screen on his smartphone. Instead of getting on, he stepped aside and used his long arm to block the sensor in the doors to let the elderly couple who stood behind him get onto the elevator before the metal doors slid shut while he was preoccupied with his phone. The couple stared at him before the doors closed, intrigued by how very tall he was and wondered if the dark-skinned man was a professional basketball player. If he was, they didn't recognize him. He noticed their lingering interest in him but he was used to being the object of people's curiosity so he winked at them before the elevator doors closed and then turned his attention back to his incoming call. He wanted to hear what had transpired that night and feared that he might lose the cell signal inside the confines of the small silver box. He swiped his finger across the touchscreen and answered the phone.

"Hello Herman," Yusef said. His voice was so deep that it almost seemed like an echo that came from some far off distance.

"Goodnight Yusef. Guess what I just watched?" Herman asked on the other line.

"She actually did it?" Yusef asked, somewhat surprised.

"She sure did. It was sexy too," Herman answered.

"How'd she do it?" Yusef asked, looking around cautiously to make sure that no one in the lobby was eavesdropping on his conversation.

"Pretty easily. It was kind of disturbing too, but sexy," Herman told him.

"Yes, you said that before but HOW exactly did she do it?"

"Oh, she drugged him, tied him up and then drowned him in the bathtub after she took a shower. She left a bottle of liquor in the bathroom next to him. I guess she thinks the cops will just think he got drunk, passed out and then drowned."

"You think the police will buy that?"

"I doubt it but hey, it is what it is. Anyway, it's your turn to watch her. I'm hungry and I need something to eat," Herman told him.

"You're always hungry. I'll get on it as soon as I pay our lecherous buddy a visit. I'm in the lobby of the hotel he's staying in now. Do you have any idea where she was going?" Yusef asked.

"Well, I never got a chance to speak with her but, I'm pretty sure we both know where she's probably headed to next," Herman answered matter-of-factly as if the answer to that question should have been obvious.

"Really? You don't think she's had enough for one night? You really think she'd do THAT tonight too?"

"From what I've seen tonight, she can't wait to take care of another one. She was exhilarated and intoxicated by the satisfaction she felt after Grossman was dead. She has that hunger, that starving need for swift and immediate vengeance in her now. She won't wait," Herman explained.

"And I wonder how she became so empty and desperate to feel full?" Yusef accused.

"Don't you dare judge me," Herman laughed. "I won't have it, especially coming from you Mr. War…King Strife."

## PART 6

# THE SICK & THE DYING

After Yusef's brief chat with Herman, he stepped into the next available elevator that arrived in the lobby and rode it up to the fifteenth floor where his friend Silvio had booked a room. He strolled across the long corridor's tacky carpeting and tried to ignore the gaudy wallpaper. Yusef's actions and his demeanor were often violent and brutal but his tastes and sensibilities were surprisingly quite refined. Fortunately, it was a short walk to the room. With enormous hands and bony, gnarled knuckles, he knocked on the door. A few moments later, he heard the lock turn and stepped inside after the door opened.

Silvio was dressed in a bath robe that he might as well have not bothered to put on because he had come to the door with it untied and wide open, obviously not bashful about being naked in front of his friend. He glistened with perspiration and his long, black, greasy hair hung down wildly into his face.

"Close your damn robe. Nobody wants to see all of that," Yusef complained, annoyed but also slightly amused.

"You look stressed. Sit down, relax, have a drink," Silvio told him as he closed the hotel room door first and then his robe.

"Looks like you've had yourself a great night," Yusef said.

He looked around at the state of the place before he sat down in the chair next to the rectangular desk adjacent to the wall on the far side of the room. The wet spots on the damp linens scattered on the unmade bed made them look as if they had been caught outside in the rain. Various articles of clothing and underwear that appeared to have been discarded hastily were strewn all over the floor randomly along with empty liquor bottles.

"Yes, it's been a wild night," Silvio answered as he pulled his hair up into a ponytail to get it out of his face.

"Typical," said Yusef as he grabbed one of the plastic red cups on the desk and poured himself a shot of vodka from the only bottle that still had anything in it. He looked across at Silvio and paused before he took his first sip. "Is that make-up on your face?" he asked in disbelief, referring to the dark eye-liner and the smeared, red lipstick on Silvio's mouth.

"Oh…yeah…it is," Silvio answered, blushing as he tried to wipe off the lipstick with the sleeve of his bathrobe. "She did it…said she liked me pretty."

"Who did it?" Yusef asked, trying his best not to laugh at how ridiculous Silvio looked.

Right after he asked, Yusef heard a woman retching in the bathroom as if she was going to vomit up all of her insides along with her soul. He shook his head. In his time, he had been the orchestrator of a great deal of suffering and misery himself but he had never been fond of the games Silvio played.

"She painted me up like this," Silvio answered, pointing to the closed bathroom door as he sat down on the messy mattress.

Yusef shot him a look of disapproval before he took huge gulp of the vodka. It didn't burn his throat and no matter how much he drank, he wouldn't become intoxicated but he still enjoyed the taste.

"Is she?" Yusef started to ask but Silvio interrupted him.

"Going to die?" Silvio finished Yusef's sentence. "Of course she is. They all are. We all are...just some a lot sooner than others," he answered.

"You know exactly what I mean," he shot back sternly to counter Silvio's flippant attitude about such a grave matter. Unlike his brethren, Yusef still took certain things seriously.

"Oh, so you want to know if she's sick because of me?" Silvio asked.

"Yes."

"Well, that's a simple question I suppose but the answer is multi-layered and complicated because the actual truth is both yes, and no," Silvio answered.

"Speak plainly. I'm not in the mood for riddles," Yusef told him as he emptied what little dregs of vodka were left in the bottle into his red plastic cup.

"Yes, straightforward and to the point is the way you say you prefer but, don't pretend that you don't play your games in your own way. We all do."

"Maybe, but that doesn't answer my question. Who's the woman retching in the bathroom and what's wrong with her?"

"Her name is Brenda…or Barbie I think. I can't remember. I've been calling her 'B' all night. No, wait…I'm almost sure it's Barbie. I met her in Sensualis, the sex club across the street and for your information, she was terminally ill before I even touched her," Silvio started to explain.

"I doubt that."

"I have no reason to lie."

"Judging by the way she sounds in that bathroom right now, I find it hard to believe that they let her in the club in that condition, or that she was even like that when you first brought her up here. Are you trying to tell me that you don't have anything to do with whatever's wrong with her now?" Yusef asked, pointing his long finger in the direction of the locked bathroom door.

"Honestly, I didn't exactly say that but, let me explain. Sweet, sick and dying *Miss Barbie* that you seem to be so concerned about really isn't a good person at all and she deserves all that is about to happen to her," Silvio told him.

"Says who?" Yusef asked. He knew how cruel and malicious his friend could be and whatever end that woman was about to meet was almost certainly going to be quite horrific.

"Says me," Silvio answered with conviction.

"And how would you know that she's not a good person? When did you, of all people, become the authority on such things?" Yusef asked with a raised eyebrow.

"I know who she is, and more importantly WHAT she is because I've been following her and keeping track of her heinous misdeeds." Silvio answered.

"Which were?" Yusef asked.

"That thing…that monster in the bathroom that is undoubtedly engaged in a loving embrace with the porcelain god worshipped by drunkards and people who are full of shit, is technically a serial killer."

"Really?"

"Yes, really. You see, a few years ago, Miss Barbie's long-time boyfriend infected her with the HIV virus. He was actually living a double-life behind her back, batting and catching balls for the other side if you get my meaning but, that's beside the point. When she was diagnosed with the disease, it was like a death sentence to her. Then, it progressed into full-blown AIDs and ever since, she's been on a mission to infect as many men as she could out of pure spite. Don't be fooled though. As sick as she is, she certainly doesn't look like it. She is still a bad bitch and absolutely drop dead gorgeous. It wasn't hard for her to find new victims. That's for damn sure. You should see the body on her too…every man's wet dream. Trust me, I had a lot of fun with her as you can see by the state of things in here," Silvio snickered. "Now, I see the way you're looking at me but, before you judge me, know that I gave her every opportunity to make me change my mind about what I had planned for her. I was sweet and kind…a gentleman even, hoping that she would feel bad, show mercy and change her mind about what she had planned for ME. I tried to use protection but she insisted that I didn't. She said she wanted to feel me inside her without the condom…even claimed to be allergic to the latex. So, we had unprotected, raw, kinky sex and now she's in the bathroom dying with her face in the toilet."

"She doesn't sound all that different from you," Yusef joked. "But, I suppose you have the exclusive rights to spread plagues and disease."

"That I do. I mean, I am Pestilence incarnate after all. Am I not?"

They both were slightly startled when the woman Silvio referred to as "Barbie" staggered out of the bathroom, paler than the white sheets on the bed. Tears of blood streaked down her face. Also, some sort of awful, thick, yellow muck formed at the corners of her mouth and her hands trembled uncontrollably. Yusef saw past all of that and realized that Silvio had absolutely told the truth about the buxom blonde's beauty. If not for the onslaught of mysterious maladies that she had been infected with, she would have been absolutely ravishing. Her lips moved but only a choked, croaking sound came out of her mouth. Then, she suddenly fell forward, face-first onto the hotel room floor, dead before she landed on the coarse carpet.

"Oh well. That's that. You're going to clean up this mess I suppose?" Yusef questioned.

"Of course. I always do," Silvio answered.

"I'll leave you to it then. I'm off to keep an eye on Cali," said Yusef as he stood up to leave.

"And how is our little would-be killer?" Silvio asked.

"Not *would-be* anymore. According to Herman, she offed Chadwick Grossman earlier tonight."

"Really? And here I was, doubting that she would actually go through with it. What about the others?"

"Herman's convinced that she's going after the next one now. He doesn't think she'll let it wait. She's dying to take care of the next one. I'm sure his influence had something to do with that too."

"Well then, you better get going," said Silvio.

"Yeah, I know," Yusef answered as he stepped over Barbie's dead body on his way to the hotel room door.

# PART 7

# FLYING WITHOUT WINGS

Maria sat in the living room on her old, comfortable couch, exhausted and sore from serving bottles of overpriced liquor to men who pretended to be ballers at the club all night. After being confined in a tight corset that helped her fit into an outfit that was the equivalent of a superhero costume for hours, it felt great to lounge around her apartment in loose-fitting sweat pants and an old, stretched out T-shirt. She was sure that she had dark bruises on the soft, flesh of her butt cheeks where she has been pinched and squeezed by perverts all night. While she watched the scandalous reality show that she had DVR'd, her mother snored loudly beside her. The old woman sounded like a chainsaw chopping down trees so Maria simply turned up the volume on the television so she could hear the dialogue on the show and let the tired lady continue to sleep. Maria knew that her mother was worn out from chasing around her granddaughter all evening while she was at work. Her child's father didn't help at all so her mother was a godsend. While she worked at night, Maria's mom kept an eye on little Brianna out of love and free of charge which saved her a ton of money in babysitting fees. Besides that, it also gave her peace of mind to know that her little mama was in her grandmother's care and not with some stranger. There were too many news reports about children being killed or molested by strangers for her to feel at ease with any other arrangement.

Before long Maria's eyelids became heavy and she started to doze off. Once she finally lost the battle against sleep, her dreams started off pleasantly enough but then took a turn in a disturbing direction. She eventually woke up in a state of panic, overwhelmed by the suffocating sensation of drowning. When she finally caught her breath and stopped coughing, she heard her little mama's voice calling her from the next room.

"I'm coming baby," Maria called out from the living room as she quickly got up off the couch and hurried to the bedroom that she shared with her child. She wasn't prepared for what she would walk in on when she got there.

Maria opened the bedroom door to find her six-year-old daughter, Brianna, sitting in the open window with her legs dangling outside. Right beside her stood a strange woman who had her hand pressed firmly against the child's back, prepared to shove her to her death. Maria covered her own mouth with her hand to keep from screaming. Brianna heard the gasp that escaped her mother's lips and looked back over her shoulder at her mom who stood stupefied in the doorway.

"There you are Mommy," the little girl chuckled, happy that her mother had finally heard her calling for her.

The female intruder turned her head slowly to face Maria and the look in her eyes carried a threat that Maria had no choice but to take seriously. What that look said clearly was that if she did, or said the wrong thing, the woman would not hesitate to push her daughter out the window. Without a single word exchanged between them, that much was very clear.

"What's going on baby? Maria asked, her voice trembling terribly with fear. Tears welled up as her eyes pleaded desperately with the woman who literally held little Brianna's life in her hands.

"I'm a fairy mommy. I'm a fairy and I can fly," Brianna chirped with excitement.

"Oh, that's great. That's wonderful. But where are your wings? You need wings to fly," Maria told her while fighting not to panic or completely break down and cry.

"But the nice lady says that I don't need wings," Brianna answered.

"Of course you do. Everything that flies needs wings. Even airplanes have wings," Maria told her daughter but really, she was pleading with the woman who appeared to be poised to murder her child.

"Do I really need wings Fairy Lady?" little Brianna asked the mysterious woman.

Cali had snuck into the apartment by climbing up the fire escape that led up to Maria's mother's bedroom, then snuck down the hallway, hoping to find Maria in bed but stumbled upon Brianna instead.

Callously and without conscience, she had decided to use the child as leverage against Maria to get her right where she wanted her. With death and bad intentions in her eyes, she stared directly at Maria before she spoke again to answer Brianna's question.

"Your mom is right. You need wings to fly. She and I will go and get you some," Cali told the little girl as she stared into Maria's soul, issuing a subtle warning that her threat was very real and that it would be best if the terrified mother complied with whatever she had in mind.

Cali helped the little girl swing her dangling legs back inside and set her down safely on the ground. Then she gave Maria a nod that meant that she wanted to have words with her outside of the bedroom, out of earshot of the little girl.

"You stay right there until we get back baby," Maria told her daughter.

"Okay mommy," Brianna answered.

Nervously, Maria backed out of the room into the hallway and waited for the mysterious intruder to meet her. In her mind, she decided that she would have to fight this woman and subdue her in order to protect her child. When Cali walked out of the room to meet her like a goon, then pressed the .22 caliber pistol to her gut, all of those ideas were replaced with an overwhelming sense of doom and helplessness.

"What do you want? Why are you doing this?" Maria demanded.

"You really don't remember me do you?" Cali asked.

"I've never met you before. I don't know you. Why are you doing this? Please don't hurt my family," Maria pleaded desperately with the strange woman although, there was something vaguely familiar about the woman with the gun. She couldn't quite place where they had met before.

"Come with me to the roof so I can refresh your memory," Cali told her, then shoved her with her free hand down the narrow hallway towards the front door.

"No, I can't leave my daughter alone. Please, just leave. I won't call the police or anything. Just leave. Don't hurt my family," Maria begged.

"Let me explain something to you," Cali hissed in a hoarse whisper. "You have two options. Come with me now, or I'll shoot you in the face. After I do that, I'll shoot your old mother in the face when the sound of the gunshot wakes her up. Then I'll go right back into that bedroom and fling your six year-old out of that window. Now choose," Cali told her with such cruel conviction in her voice that Maria quietly complied.

"I hope that all of this isn't over some man," Maria said as she and Cali walked onto the roof of the apartment building through a metal door that creaked open on rusty hinges.

The night air felt unseasonably cold for that time of year and the sound of the loose gravel crunching under their feet as they walked sounded almost the same as if they tramped through freshly fallen snow.

"Actually, this is about some men…plural, but we'll get to the details of that a little later sweetheart," Cali answered. "Now move it so we can get this over with. I've had a very long night and I really need some sleep," she said and pushed Maria hard in the back to force her forward.

"Men?" Maria asked, quite surprised. "Listen, I don't know which one of your boyfriends has been flirting with me, or which ones I've been messing with but, I never knew about you. He, him, them… they never mentioned you," Maria said in a desperate attempt to reason with the woman who had a gun pointed at her.

"Oh, you've got it all wrong. I wouldn't be going through all of this trouble for something so trivial…something so petty," Cali answered.

"So why are you doing this? Why are we here?" Maria asked.

"In order for you to understand the *why* of all this, I have to make you remember me," Cali told her coldly.

"But I already told you, I don't know you. I've never met you," Maria explained again, desperately hoping to save herself from whatever came next.

"I suppose that I should be hurt, or at least bothered that you don't remember me but I'm not. If I were you, I probably would have done everything I could to forget the brief time in my life when we knew each other," said Cali.

"What are you talking about?" Maria asked, convinced that the woman who had the small caliber pistol pointed at her head was completely out of her mind.

"You know, I used to serve drinks too. I was a bottle service girl, just like you," Cali told her.

"How do you know that?" Maria asked nervously as she wondered how long this madwoman might have been stalking her.

"They said I was pretty," Cali continued, ignoring Maria's question for the moment. "They said I had a nice body and that I could earn a lot of money at the club. I wanted to sing. They said that I could meet celebrities, established people in the music business if I worked in the club. So, I worked in the club. I made a lot of friends at the club, or at least people who pretended to be my friends. I met Chadwick Grossman at the club."

"What does Chad have to do with this?" Maria asked, visibly more agitated and alarmed than before.

"He had a lot to do with all of this, but, I'll get to that in a second," Cali answered with an intense stare that was so filled with hate that Maria's blood ran ice cold. "Let me ask you a question…that little girl downstairs in your apartment, your beautiful daughter, Chadwick was the father wasn't he?" Cali asked.

"How can you know that? No one knows that," Maria asked, filled with disbelief and dread.

"It's the eyes. She has her father's eyes," Cali answered.

"And why did you ask if he *was* her father? What's happened to him? What have you done?" Maria asked after feeling a horrible sinking feeling in her gut that something terrible had happened.

"Around the time when we knew each other, a time in your life that I'm sure you forgot on purpose, I remember when you invited me to have a few drinks with Chadwick and one of his new artists. You said that if they heard me sing, they might even put me on a record. I was so stupid back then because I actually believed you," Cali told her, and watched as old forgotten memories came rushing back with full force into Maria's mind.

"No, you can't be? That's impossible," she started before Cali continued to jog her memory.

"They didn't want to hear me sing. They only wanted to fuck. You let them fuck you but when I didn't let them touch me, they forced me, they raped me, and they made me scream instead. Do you remember watching them make me scream? I know you do. I remember that you watched everything. You never turned away. When they covered my mouth, I begged you to help me with my eyes. You didn't and you never looked away."

"No, no, no. You can't be her. That's impossible. You can't be Sta---," Maria started to say, finally figuring out who the woman with the gun REALLY was but again, Cali cut her off.

"Don't say that name. That's not who I am anymore and as far as you're concerned, tonight my name is Death!" Cali yelled as she took two steps closer to Maria.

"Please don't do this. I'm so sorry. I couldn't stop them. Please don't do this," Maria pleaded as she slowly retreated towards the ledge at the edge of the rooftop.

When she ran out of space to back up, Maria looked over her shoulder, over the edge of the high-rise apartment building and felt nauseous from the dizzying height. When she turned her eyes away from the unforgiving concrete sidewalk hundreds of feet below, Cali was chest to chest with her and pressed the pistol firmly under her chin.

"You asked me about Chadwick before and genuinely sounded concerned. I don't know why. It's not like he gave a shit about you, or even acknowledged your baby. But, I feel sorry for your child because no one should lose two parents in the same night," Cali said through gritted teeth.

"No, don't," she pleaded just before Cali shoved her backwards and over the side of the roof.

Maria's screams pierced the quiet of the night like the shrieking of a car's brakes right before a traffic accident.

In his car, Yusef slowly circled the block where Maria lived as he waited patiently for Cali to show up. He eventually grew tired of wasting gas and was just about to look for a parking space when he heard the scream from above. He rolled down his tinted window and looked up just in time to see Maria hurtle to the ground like a flailing, uncoordinated angel before her body hit the pavement and exploded like rotten fruit.

# PART 8
# THE LAW

The next night, Cali wore a long, black dress that hugged every one of her curves in honor of the two souls she had sent plummeting to the afterlife just a few hours before. She also wore one of her black, jeweled carnival masks although she certainly did not regret, or mourn either of her victim's passing. She was in the middle of slipping into her sexy, lace stockings when someone knocked gently on her dressing room door. She fixed her clothes, sat back in her chair and started to put the last hairpins in her hair to ensure that it stayed styled the way she wanted it during her performance. Then she walked over to the door and unlocked it.

"Hey Cali," Seerule greeted her as he entered the dressing room and shut the door behind him.

"Hi," she answered pleasantly as she turned away from him to return to her swivel chair and her mirror. "It's not quite show time yet," she said, surprised to see him there so early.

"I know. That's not why I'm here," he told her, sounding a bit worried and troubled at the same time.

"What's wrong?" she asked, noticing the look on his face when she looked at his reflection in the mirror as he stood behind her and seemed to purposely keep his distance.

"I'm not sure how to say this," he began.

"Just spit it out. Don't worry, I'm a hard woman to offend. It's smooth as silk but I have very thick skin," she said as she playfully lifted up her skirt to show him some thigh.

"Well, what I have to say is not the sort of thing you just blurt out," he told her.

"Blurt it out anyway," she said, becoming as serious as he was at the moment.

"What happened last night, after you and Chadwick left?" he asked.

"I'm not sure if that's any of your business," she answered sternly, assuming that the question had been prompted by some latent jealousy he felt because of the crush he obviously had on her.

"I'm being serious. What happened exactly?" he asked again.

"And like I said before, it's not really your business," she answered again, spinning around in the swivel chair so that she could face him.

"Listen, don't get the wrong idea. I'm not trying to be all up in your business. I'm trying to help you."

"Help me? Help me how?"

"Right now, there's a detective Bronson in Gabriel's office asking questions about his buddy, Chadwick," Seerule explained.

"A detective? Asking questions? What kind of questions? What did Chadwick do last night?" she asked, feigning ignorance.

"It's not what he did. It's what got done to him," he explained.

"What got done to him? What're you talking about?" she asked, pretending to be shocked, appalled and concerned.

"They found him in his own bathtub this morning...dead...drowned. It almost looked like an accident but the detective says that there's evidence that his hands were bound at some point. You know anything about that?"

"Who knows what kind of kinky shit that man was into?" she asked, annoyed as she turned away from him and continued to fix her hair in the mirror.

"You sure you weren't the one playing the kinky games with him?" Seerule asked.

"Of course not! You think I'm one of the sluts and whores that works here?" she yelled, genuinely offended.

"That's not what I said, or implied. But, the boss and I both know that you left with him last night. That's why I'm here asking you to tell me the truth, before the detective makes his way down here. Tell me what happened...and I want the truth so I can help you. If you're guilty of anything bad, you need to tell me now, before it's too late," he pleaded with her.

"The truth is, after we left he tried to get me back to his apartment. I refused and he got mad. I got out of his car, not even ten blocks from here, and caught a cab home. That's the truth. So, if someone ended up playing BDSM a little too rough with the boss's boy, I suggest you tell that detective to start interviewing one of the bottle service bitches that work here. They're always eager to do something strange for some change if the money is right. And we both know that Chadwick's money was right."

"I guess. Okay, and speaking of bottle service girls, Maria jumped off the roof of her building and committed suicide last night," Seerule told her and waited for her reaction.

"Doesn't sound or seem like just a coincidence to me. Maybe she had something to do with Chadwick's death and couldn't live with what she had done, or whatever happened at his place," she stated matter-of-factly as if it all made perfect sense, connecting dots that led any suspicions far away from her.

"Maybe. That detective seems kind of incompetent though. He looks like a lush and I smelled rum on his breath. Whatever happened to those two, I doubt he'd be the guy to solve that riddle, if there really is a connection," Seerule said, wanting to believe her theory but completely conflicted by the gut feeling that fueled his suspicions.

"I guess we'll just have to wait to see if Detective Bronson is worth the metal his badge is made of," she said nonchalantly.

"I guess we will," Seerule answered. "I expect that he'll be here knocking on your door soon. I'll be back to get you when it's show time."

"See you later alligator," she said pleasantly as he left.

Cali turned her focus back to her mirror and fixing her hair as if there was no possibility that she might become the prime suspect in a double homicide once Detective Bronson showed up for a chat.

"Hello…Cali is it?" Detective Bronson greeted her, mispronouncing her name the same way that Chadwick Grossman had the night before.

The man was just as Seerule had described him. He reeked of alcohol and his brown business suit was at least a size too big. His shoes were scuffed and had definitely seen better days. The grizzled stubble on his chin was a clear indication that he cared very little for keeping himself well-groomed. In fact, his appearance was so disheveled and sloppy that it didn't seem genuine at all to her. Behind his dark eyes and furrowed brow, she sensed that a keen intellect lurked, waiting to snare her in a trap. His physical condition and appearance might very well have been a ruse, meant to distract and confuse. She remained on guard and decided that she would not fall for it.

"It's *Kah-Lee*," she corrected him.

"Oh, I apologize Cali," he said, pronouncing it right the second time around. "I know you have a show in a few minutes so I won't take up too much of your time."

"I would appreciate that. Now, what's going on?"

"Straight to the point. I like that. Well, I'm investigating what I believe to be a homicide," he answered.

"Who's dead?" Cali asked.

"Chadwick Grossman," the detective answered dryly, watching her and waiting for her reaction, much in the same way that Seerule had a few minutes earlier but somehow, she sensed that he was a much more skilled judge of character.

"And what would that have to do with me?" she asked.

"Well, one of the girls, one I won't name for obvious reasons, this being a murder investigation and all, says that she caught a glimpse of you leaving with him last night," he informed her.

"Yeah, I bet one of those bitches would say that," she snapped.

"And why is that?"

"Because none of them like me. And because they don't like the fact that their friend's child's father seemed interested in me," she said.

"Wait a minute. Back up a bit. Who? What? And why?" he asked.

"Maria's daughter is Chadwick Grossman's child, although he never owned up to it or claimed it. Check the kid's DNA. You'll see," she explained. "All of these little bitches around here are friends with Maria but none of them like me though. I guess they don't like the fact that I don't have to get pinched, squeezed and disrespected all night to make a dollar."

"Maria Calderon? The bottle service girl that also worked here, the same one that committed suicide last night?" he asked, seeming quite surprised by the connection she had just fed him.

"Yes, her," Cali answered.

"Hmmm…interesting," he said as he jotted something down in the little black notepad in his hand. "Thanks for that bit of info but, I also noticed something," he continued.

"And what's that?" Cali asked.

"You still didn't answer my first question. Did you leave here with Chad Grossman last night?" he asked.

For a split second, Cali contemplated lying but there was no way for her to be sure if the club's owner, Gabriel, or maybe even Seerule, hadn't already told him the truth. For all she knew, he might have also been inclined to trust the mysterious, anonymous source he chose not to reveal to her.

"I did leave with him. We were supposed to discuss the future of my career and a record deal for me," Cali answered truthfully.

"Sounds plausible. I can believe that. I've heard that you're an amazing singer," he said.

"You should stick around for the show," Cali invited him in an attempt to deflect any more questions.

"I just might take you up on that. But first, I've got to ask just a few more questions. I'm sorry. Okay, so after you left with him, what happened next?" Detective Bronson continued to press.

"Not even two blocks from here, he tried to get in my panties. I told him to let me out," she lied.

"And did he? I mean, he just gave up and let you out of the car, just like that?" Bronson asked.

"Of course he did," she answered.

"And you really weren't tempted to let him have his way? Wow," he said, sounding a bit surprised.

"What's so unbelievable about that?" she asked.

"You're a morally strong woman. Most girls would do anything that Chadwick Grossman, or any man like him asked just to get a shot at a major record deal."

"I'm not most girls," she answered.

"No, you definitely are not," he said before he slipped her a business card. "If you think of anything else that might be helpful, feel free to reach out to me and I'll be in touch with you if I have any more questions."

"Okay," she answered as she watched him turn and walk away.

"Break a leg miss. Have a great show," he said before closing the dressing room door behind him, leaving her alone with thoughts of what her next move should be.

## PART 9

# BALL & CHAIN

Detective Bronson's phone vibrated relentlessly in his pocket as he watched Cali's performance in a dark corner of the club. He had decided to stick around for her show just as she had suggested but not entirely for the entertainment. He remained low key and blended in with the patrons of the night club as best he could so that he could observe the behavior of the employees to see if he could pick up on anything strange. Unfortunately, he had also promised his wife that he would have been home in time for dinner so the more his phone rang and the longer he took to answer it was the more hot water he knew he was going to be in. Eventually he made his way to the men's room so that he could touch base with his anxious wife, the love of his life.

"Where are you? Why haven't you been answering my calls? And why is it so loud in there?" Mrs. Bronson screeched into the phone.

"Betty, I'm working a case," Detective Bronson explained as he stepped into the nearest empty bathroom stall.

"Working a case? So why am I hearing loud music in the background? Charlie, I swear, if you're at some seedy titty bar while I'm home with these kids," she

51

threatened, very close to going nuclear as only she could.

"I'm not at a strip club. I'm in a nightclub and I'm in the middle of a murder investigation," he answered although he doubted that she would find the truth to be much better than her accusation.

"Charles, you promised me that you would be home at a reasonable hour to help me with OUR kids but here I am, alone with three toddlers who are suffering from the flu! I need you here, right now!" she yelled into the phone.

"What I'm doing is important. This is my job. You knew that when you married me," he reminded her.

"Your family is important too. Remember when we agreed on that, when you proposed, right before I said yes? I'm not going to be doing this alone, and if you're going to force me to by never being here, then I'm really going to just decide to do it on my own," she threatened, her voice filled with frustration. Even over the telephone he could hear that she was on the brink of tears.

"I'll leave now and head home right away," he promised after hearing the distress in her voice.

"Thank you," Betty said with an attitude while still sounding slightly relieved. "And can you stop at the pharmacy and pick up some children's flu medicine? We're almost out," she requested.

"Sure thing. See you soon," Detective Bronson told his wife before he hung up.

When he finally emerged from behind the door of the bathroom stall, a young man was at one of the sinks, washing his hands.

"The old ball and chain can be a pain huh?" he asked the disheveled detective playfully.

The young man had heard the tail end of the conversation and decided to exercise one of those unwritten guy code rules. So, as a service to his fellow man, he offered the haggard, married man an opportunity to vent without judgment on his part. Detective Bronson accepted and appreciated the gesture.

"Yeah, she sure can be," he answered and walked out of the bathroom.

On the drive home, Bronson tried to mentally prepare himself for the madness he was about to walk into once he entered his humble abode in the suburbs just outside the city. Although he had headed straight home after she called him, only stopping to get the medicine for his sons, he still expected Betty to go ballistic for at least the first few minutes after he arrived. He would have to listen to her vent and rant about all of the horrors she had faced that day while caring for three cranky, noisy, demanding, overactive, sick, six year-olds. For her, he was sure that it had been torture times three and she would certainly do everything she could to make sure that he fully understood her pain.

When they were newlyweds, they hadn't exactly planned to have that many kids but, when they struggled to become pregnant after three years of trying vigorously and enthusiastically, they sought the help of a fertility specialist. Fortunately, Betty found herself with child soon after but, the drugs that the doctor had prescribed worked so well that the Bronsons ended up having triplets. Because they had prayed long, hard and passionately for a child, they couldn't complain about being blessed with three at one time but the financial burden was more than they were prepared for. When the pressure of keeping the electricity on and his family fed, Charles had no choice but to occasionally turn to shadier means in order to earn extra cash. In fact, it wasn't long after his children were born and his struggles became very real when he first met Chadwick Grossman. During a missing persons investigation he had been paid handsomely to make certain suspicions fade and make certain articles of incriminating evidence simply disappear into thin air. It was a dark misdeed, a horrible thing that still haunted the detective's thoughts years later. After the cash had been placed into his corrupt hands, he did unscrupulous things to cover up a disgusting, loathsome crime. Because of what he had helped to hide, a young woman who had been savagely raped and brutally beaten would never be found, her family would never have closure and her soul would never find rest because the atrocities committed against her would never be avenged.

Despite the unpleasant certainty of verbal spousal abuse and the incessant nagging he was moments away from facing, he drove home with a light heart. With his former associate, Chadwick Grossman, laid out on a cold slab in the city morgue with lungs full of bath water, he felt free from a piece of his shameful past. The secret that had been eating away at him for a little over half a decade had finally died with the man who had purchased Charlie Bronson's soul with a large bag of cash.

Silvio chewed pink bubblegum and watched Detective Bronson pull into the driveway of his quaint, suburban home. In the darkness, hidden in the shadows, he sat on a wooden swing attached to the oak tree at the side of the house with old rope and watched the weary man exit his car. Silvio blew a large pink bubble as the man sighed and rolled his eyes as he prepared to open his own front door. After a quick prayer, Bronson stepped inside. The mysterious flu that the detective's young sons suffered from was of course Silvio's doing. His intention was not to kill the children though. That night, he only meant to make them sick. As juicy as the conflict that was about to arise inside might have been, he was more interested in the car that would show up near the house an hour after detective Bronson arrived. For a while, Silvio almost thought that Cali wouldn't show up. He was ecstatic when she didn't disappoint him.

The children finally fell asleep thanks in part to the cold medicine that made them drowsy. They also happened to be exhausted from running their poor mother ragged all day. Charlie Bronson was well aware of the extent of the mischief they had gotten into because Betty had given him graphic, highly detailed account of it all for two hours straight with colorful language mixed in to express her displeasure. By the time she was done, he had a headache that threatened to break open his skull and he realized that hunting down murderers might really have been an easier job than being a good husband. He wasn't even sure if he was that. On most days, he debated whether or not he was even a good man.

Once Betty Bronson had griped and complained herself into a state of complete exhaustion, most of the frustration she felt left her system. After that, they both went off to bed. She fell asleep right away but he was still restless, plagued by the odd circumstances of Chadwick Grossman's death and Maria Calderon's apparent suicide. The dots of both cases seems easy enough to connect based on the obvious connections but he couldn't shake the feeling that some crucial bit of information was still missing. Eventually, the unsolved mystery drove him out of his bed and out of the house entirely.

Detective Bronson smoked a cigarette at the edge of the lake behind his house. His wife would have bitched and moaned if she found out because she had begged him to quit a thousand times. For the most part, he had but every now and then, a Newport 100 or two relaxed him and helped to clear his mind, an important thing for a man whose job it was to solve murder mysteries. He was so engrossed in his own thoughts that he never heard anyone walk up behind him. He only realized that he wasn't alone when a heavy, blunt object struck him in the back of his head. Then everything went black.

Charlie Bronson woke up, bound tightly by heavy chains and barely able to move. Once his vision cleared and he caught his bearings, he realized that he was flat on his back in the small rowboat that he sometimes used to go fishing on the tiny lake. He assumed that the woman that sat in the boat with him was the one who had struck him down and tied him up.

"Who are you?" he asked groggily.

"I'm nobody. Just a dead girl that most of the world forgot," Cali answered.

"You can't be a dead girl. You seem very alive to me," he said.

"If I told you who I was, I doubt you'd feel that way." she answered as she continued to row the boat towards the middle of the calm, murky body of water.

"So, who are you?" Bronson asked. "There's something familiar about you."

"Well, that's because you questioned me in my dressing room earlier tonight when I was getting ready for my show."

"Cali?" he asked in disbelief as his eyes opened wide. When he had spoken to her earlier at the club, her face had been concealed by her black, masquerade mask but now that he looked closely, her recognized her eyes.

"Yes, that's my name, the one I gave myself and the one that everyone calls me but, who I really am is something entirely different," she explained, then flashed a smile that made the seasoned policeman's blood turn to ice.

"Why are you doing this?" he asked.

"I think you know why or, at least you already know part of the *why* of all this," Cali answered.

"You had something to do with Grossman's death didn't you?"

"I had more than something to do with Chadwick's departure from this life. I was the one who tied him up, drugged him, then drowned him," she confessed.

"And what about young Miss Calderon? Did Maria really commit suicide or did you have a hand in that too?" he asked.

"Yes, I flung her from that rooftop," she confessed again nonchalantly.

"You said that this isn't really who you are," he said as he struggled to somehow find a way to slip free of the chains. He knew that there was very little chance that she intended to let him live after she had just confessed to two different murders. If he had any hope at all of not being her next victim, he needed to figure out what kind of psychological breakdown was driving her actions. "If you're not the sweet singer who I interviewed earlier, who are you then?" he asked.

"I'm not crazy or insane detective. I am Cali, the singer from Club Xplosive but, I'm also something else," she answered.

"What are you talking about?"

"I am a dead girl, living a second life. I was the girl that Chad and his friends raped and murdered. They dumped my body down a sewer. No one ever knew what happened to me, except for them...and YOU. I'm not exactly sure what I am NOW but, to answer your first question, for tonight I am absolutely going to be the last face you will ever see!"

Detective Bronson and held his breath for as long as he could as he sunk to the bottom of the lake. He looked up and saw the pale, full moon clearly as it glowed like an enormous pearl in the sea of the black sky, even from his point of view underneath the murky waters. Bound and weighted the way that he was, wrapped in chains along with the cinder block Cali had tied his feet to, he knew that he was a dead man for certain. His body would sit at the bottom of the lake, probably never to be found, and his wife would assume that he had run off. His sons would falsely believe that he had abandoned them. That was what he found most tragic about the way he was about to meet his end. After what he had done, he supposed he deserved it but we he would have much rather been gunned down in the line of duty for the world to see, so that the people he left behind would have had something to be proud of. If he had a choice in the matter, he would have begged for a hero's death for the sake of his family, even if it was a lie. He closed his eyes and began to swallow water.

"Well damn, she really is deadly and ruthless indeed," Silvio mumbled to himself as he stood in the shadows of the tree line, a few feet away from the shores of the lake as he watched Cali slowly row the boat back towards dry land. "What a beautifully dangerous and delicious creature."

## PART 10
# THE LAST SHOW

ali sat in front of the mirror in her dressing room with tears of joy streaming down her cheeks. Her black mascara ran and resembled war paint on the sides of her face. She smiled as she stared at the mask on the make-up table in front of her that she wasn't going to wear for her final performance at the club that night because she was going to step out onto the stage, under the bright lights as no one else but herself, exactly what she had become. The, she heard someone knock on her dressing room door.

"Come in," Cali yelled and then listened to the door creak open slowly. "You know, I thought I was going to have to hunt you down," Cali said to the man behind her who had just entered her dressing room upon her request.

Mike Down, better known as *Skil Kraft the Rapper*, stood at the door with a smug grin, full of gold teeth. Ever since his career had taken off, the one thing he still couldn't believe was the way women from all walks of life gave themselves to him so easily, with very little effort on his part. He was not a very handsome man, nor was he particularly witty outside of the lyrics in his music or charming so it hadn't always been like that for him but because of his fame, his sex life was very good.

"A fly bitch like you never has to hunt me down. All you gotta do is holla," he answered with his version of flattery.

"I've been waiting so long to get a chance to be in the same room with you that this doesn't even feel real," she said, overcome with emotion as she stared at the seven knives laid out on the vanity in front of her. From where Mike was standing behind her with his back against the dressing room door, he couldn't see them or how sharp they were.

"I gotta admit, I was a little surprised when Gabriel told me that you wanted to meet me so bad that you asked him to tell me to come down to your dressing room. You have a reputation for being a diva around here. They say you're a stuck up bitch," he said.

"Really? Is that what they say?" she asked, pretending to sound surprised. "Well, now that you're here with me, what do you think?"

"I think that we should get right to what you got me down here for," he answered and started to unbuckle his five hundred-dollar belt.

"Me too," she answered as she skillfully gathered all seven of the knives she was about to introduce him to.

When Cali spun around in the swivel chair to face him, he didn't hear a gunshot so he wondered where the excruciating pain in his right shoulder had come from. It was only when he turned his head to look that he understood what had happened, even though he struggled to believe it. She had moved so fast that he hadn't seen her throw it but there was a knife embedded deep enough in his flesh to almost pin him to the door like a poster. His first instinct was to reach for the doorknob but just as he did, another knife pierced his left hand and nailed it to the door as well.

"What the fuck!" he yelled in agony and shock.

"Don't scream again or I swear I'll put the next one through your eye," she threatened.

Mike clenched his teeth so that he wouldn't scream when the next two knives she threw stabbed him in his right and left thigh. Blood leaked from his body and pooled up on the floor at his feet as she used him as a human dart board. He raised his right hand to beg her to stop but as soon as he exposed his palm, she let another blade fly and pinned that hand to the back of the door as well.

"Please stop," he whimpered weakly as he became light headed and wasn't sure how much more torture he could take.

"I remember begging you like that once," she said as she slowly walked towards him with the last two knives in her hand. "I asked your friend Chad, and I asked YOU to *please stop* but you didn't."

"I…don't…know…what you're talking about," he answered as his pulse raced so wildly that he thought he might die of a heart attack way before he blacked out from blood loss.

"Oh, you don't? You don't remember a silly singer girl who wanted to sing you a song, so desperate and excited to have a chance to maybe get on a record with you that she didn't see the danger she had put herself in? You don't remember holding her down, ripping off her clothes, beating her, taking turns raping her and listening to her scream for mercy…begging for it to be over? I bet you don't remember her passing out…or how you all panicked when you thought she was dead. Do you even remember where you dumped her body?"

"You can't be her," he said in disbelief as he shut his eyes and refused to look at her.

In a rage, Cali drove the next to last knife in her hands deep into the wood of the door right next to his head, just inches away from his skull.

"Open your eyes and look at me so that you know that I was that silly singer girl!" she yelled.

Mike reluctantly raised his eyelids and looked directly at her. Once she saw in his eyes and in his soul that he recognized her, she smiled. Then, she knew that the time had come for her to grant him what she had given all of the other unfortunate souls whose names had also been scribbled on her death list…DEATH.

With her last knife, Cali viciously stabbed Mike in the sternum. Then, she slowly dragged the blade downwards and ripped him open from chest to crotch. That's how she left him, with his entrails dangling out of his body as she went to perform her final show, without her mask for the first time and with her hands covered in blood.

# PART 11
# THE GATHERING

Nightclubs are very unique places. Whether they stood underneath the overhead strobe lights where they wanted to be seen or in the dark corners where they desired to hide, people patronized clubs to live out some of their wildest, exciting fantasies freely. Surrounded by strangers within those walls, folks often transformed into what they truly were as they drowned in a sea of lively bodies and loud music. Places that combined an overabundance of libations and extremely suggestive sensuality always formed a nexus for the gathering of powerful forces. The product of sex is life and life itself is the polar opposite of death. The conflict between those two primal forces is a battle that will only see its conclusion at the end of all things.

Herman had been the first to arrive. After he flashed a large sum of cash at the door, he had been escorted to one of the fancy VIP sections of the nightclub and given complimentary bottles of liquor, courtesy of the club owner. While he waited for his friends to arrive, he started to drink alone. His thoughts kept drifting back to unpleasant events from earlier in the day when he had let two children who had been abandoned by their junkie parents starve to death. Considering their predicament, he thought it was a merciful end to what would have otherwise been a tormented, tortuous life for the little ones. But, his guilt stemmed from the reality that he was also responsible for the gaping hole in the neglectful parents' souls that no matter how hard they tried, or how high they got, could never be filled. A small part of him, the tiny bit of humanity that still lingered, caused him to feel a slight hint of remorse like a splinter that he couldn't remove, no matter how hard he tried. The emptiness that constantly consumed him caused Herman to attempt to become as intoxicated as possible so that he could at least be temporarily be relieved of that small bit of guilt. He had been cursed to infect others with his insatiable hunger. It was a heavy burden because he still had a conscience, something he wished he could be rid of. In order for him to feel full, he had to make others feel empty and as selfish as that was, he had no idea how to end it.

## - FAMINE

"A man like you looks like you could use some sexy female company. "You need some sugar?" Trixie the dancer asked as she snuggled up next to Silvio. She had a thing for the well-dressed, dashing, handsome ones.

"A man like me you said? Sweetheart, there are no men like me...not in this world...I promise you," Silvio said before he leaned forward and gave her a sweet, soft, peck on the cheek. Then he pushed Trixie away and sent her on about her business while he looked for Herman.

A strange thing happened to Trixie afterwards as she roamed through the club and fished for tips. She began to cough uncontrollably and her nose started to run. Sweat beaded up on her forehead and her body felt as if it was on fire inside from a deadly fever. Suddenly, she became light-headed and stumbled forward on shaky legs. Colette, one of the bottle service girls, caught her arm just before she would have fallen flat on her face.

"Hey Girl. Damn, you look so pale. Are you alright?" Collette asked, genuinely concerned.

"I don't know what's wrong with me. I felt fine when I came in to work. Now I feel like I'm coming down with the worst flu I've ever had in my life," Trixie answered.

"You should go and ask Seerule if you can have the rest of the night off," Colette suggested as she helped Trixie to steady herself.

"I can't. I've taken off too many days this month already and I need the..."

Trixie was going to say "money" before her body went limp and she collapsed on the floor.

"Oh my god! Somebody help!" Colette yelled.

She reached down to touch Trixie's hand and found that it was ice cold. The gorgeous exotic dancer who had seemed fine just twenty minutes before now convulsed erratically on the club floor as she suffered from some sort of seizure.

# - PESTILENCE

"Is that girl going to die?" Herman asked as Silvio sat down next to him in the VIP section.

"No, I'm feeling merciful tonight. She'll just spend a few days in the hospital and if the doctors who care for her are any good, she'll be right as rain in a week or two," Silvio answered and flashed a wicked grin.

"That doesn't sound like mercy," Herman laughed as he raised his glass to toast his friend.

"And how many empty bellies and starving souls have you left in your wake lately?" Silvio asked with a raised eyebrow.

"It's funny that you ask. Now THAT is an interesting story," Herman started to reply.

"Wait. Hold that thought," Silvio stopped him after he noticed a wild commotion at the main bar. "I think Yusef just arrived."

A massive, six-man brawl had erupted at the main bar. There was cursing, punches being thrown and one of the men involved got a bottle of champagne smashed over the top of his head. The burly bouncers rushed in and tried as best they could to contain the fight before it spilled over onto the main floor. If it did, the violence and panic that ensued would be impossible to get under control. Then, out of the chaos, Herman and Silvio saw Yusef appear. He walked through the middle of the madness towards them as relaxed as a man out for a quiet, evening stroll.

"Is that your doing?" Silvio asked, pointing to the ruckus where the club's security had just barely started to restore some semblance of order.

"Of course," Yusef laughed heartily.

"You couldn't resist could you?" Herman asked and handed Yousef a bottle of champagne as he joined them at their small, round table.

"Of course not. I couldn't help myself. It's my nature," he answered unapologetically. "Besides, why should you two villains be the only ones who get to have fun?"

"What did you do?" Silvio asked.

"Nothing much. Just nudged them a bit. A bit of testosterone, aggression, jealousy and pride mixed just right and before you know it, you've got yourself a nice, heated conflict that hopefully turns into a violent fight," Yusef told them.

- WAR

Not a single band member played a single note when Cali stepped out onto the stage without a mask on, dressed in a long white gown that was covered in what appeared to be fresh blood. It was the first time any of them had seen her face but it was the blood on her hands that had caught their attention. She ignored the stunned looks and walked to the microphone that was cradled in the tall, metal stand close to the edge of the stage.

With the band still locked in a state of complete shock, Cali sang her last song acapella and her voice had never been more soulful. She sang with genuine pain that resonated throughout the hearts of everyone that heard her and for a brief moment that none in attendance would ever forget, they all felt her pain intimately. The lyrics of the ballad she shared vividly described the tragedy of innocence lost at the hands of wicked men, and being betrayed by the indifference of a woman who could have saved her. By the time her song was done, no one, not even the most heartless person in attendance, remain unmoved. There were some in the crowd who even wept. Three men who sat in the VIP section drinking together paid particularly close attention.

"Seems like she might be the one," said Herman.

"I don't often see eye-to-eye with you fat boy but this time, I have to admit that I'm leaning towards agreeing with you," said Silvio.

"We're all familiar with what she represents. It's undeniable. Besides, I'd like some female company for a change. I'm really getting tired of our little three amigos sausage-fest," added Yusef.

"Well then, in that case, let's go introduce ourselves to our new little sister," said Silvio.

and her name was... - DEATH

# PART 12
# INTRODUCTIONS

Cali calmly sat alone in her dressing room, still wearing her white gown that was stained with blood. Without a drop of fear, she waited patiently for the sounds of wailing sirens, scratchy walkie-talkies and policemen's boots pounding the floor on the other side of the door where a superstar rapper's body was still pinned like a poster. His blood had formed a thick, crimson puddle at his feet which had spread and leaked under the door, out into the hallway. Cali was shocked that no one had noticed it and come knocking yet. When she finally heard footsteps on the other side of the door, she took a deep breath and mentally prepared herself for whatever would happen next but, what happened next wasn't anything that a normal person would expect.

Three very unusual men strolled into the room and shut the door behind them nonchalantly, as if there wasn't a corpse with knives sticking out of it nailed to the door. The heavyset, huskiest of the three stayed by the door while the other two casually walked towards Cali. The handsome, long-haired, pale one sat on the makeup table while the unusually tall, dark and ruggedly handsome one pulled up a chair beside her. In their presence, Cali sensed that there was

71

something inherently terrifying about the trio but she was not terrified. In fact, she felt surprisingly at ease.

"You know, most people hang their coats, or hats, or even scarves on the back of doors…not dead bodies," said the tall, dark-skinned stranger that sat beside her. He had kind, dark brown eyes but there was an eerie fire that burned behind them.

"Who are you and what are all of you doing in my dressing room?" Cali asked.

"Who we are is…complicated. But, let's keep things simple for now. My name is Yusef. The pretty one sitting on your make-up table is Silvio and the nice gentleman at the door is Herman," Yusef answered.

"Okay, so…Yusef, Silvio and Herman…what are you doing here?" Cali asked.

"Good question but, what the REAL question of the hour is, what are YOU still doing here?" Yusef asked.

"Waiting," Cali answered.

"Waiting for what?" Herman asked. He had not taken his eyes off of the dead body since he walked in. He continued to stare at it and study it as if it was a gruesome painting made of flesh.

"Waiting for whatever comes next," she answered.

"And what do you think comes next?" Silvio asked as he smiled at her and straightened his man bun which had become slightly unraveled. In his eyes, she truly was a deadly, beautiful creature.

"I don't know. I'm just sitting here waiting to find out," she answered.

"Well, if you just sit here, I can tell you what happens next," said Yusef. "Before long, someone besides the three of us will discover what you've done. They'll call men to put you in handcuffs and those men will see to it that you stay locked up, probably forever. To me, that's a shame, a waste and practically a sin."

"More sinful than the things I've done?" she asked sarcastically.

"Yes. Absolutely. And I can't possibly imagine you wasting away in a cage because you chose to sit here waiting for them to come for you without my heart breaking," Yusef answered.

"Well that's too bad I guess. I don't see how else this plays out," said Cali.

"And what if I told you that there was another way…a different path that you could choose?" Yusef asked.

"And what path is that?" Cali asked, somewhat curious but mostly suspicious.

"Come with us and find out," Silvio answered before Yusef could.

"No thank you. The last time I went somewhere with strange men who made empty promises, I ended up discarded like a piece of garbage and very dead," she answered.

"We don't want to hurt you and we can't kill. No, I don't think we could kill you, even if we tried," Yusef answered.

"Besides, we've seen what you did to the ones who hurt you in your *other life*. We wouldn't want to end up on your *list*," Herman added from across the room.

"You should really come with us," said Silvio as he gently touched Cali's chin. "So we can show you what you are…and maybe what you could become."

# PART 13
# RED HOSTESS

ali woke up in a strange bed, in a bedroom that wasn't hers and barely remembered how she got there. Through a hazy mental fog, she recalled how she had casually and calmly fled her dressing room, the scene of her latest crime, with three very unusual men, none of whom seemed to have bothered her while she slept. She realized how reckless and potentially foolish it might have been to put so much trust in three individuals that she knew so little about but, that's exactly what she had done, regardless of the risk. She had no doubt that they were all very dangerous but, as she discovered since her new life began, so was she. Strangely enough, she also felt stronger in the presence of the odd trio than she had ever felt on her own.

On the far end of the room stood an enormous, oak wardrobe that resembled a menacing golem carved out of wood. The look of it clashed with the modern décor of the rest of the room and made it seem completely out of place. It stood out like some antique, magical thing that had somehow survived from a time when people believed in such things. There were intricate, highly-detailed images and strange words carved deeply into its surface. Although she didn't know their meaning or significance, Cali felt the power in the shapes, symbols and images. At the very top of it, there were two oval-shaped cut-outs that eerily resembled empty eye-sockets. Her blood-stained gown hung neatly on a hanger, hooked securely over one of the knobs on one of the wardrobe's double-doors.

Cali pulled back the sheets and realized that she was dressed in comfortable men's pajamas that were a few sizes too big for her. She didn't remember putting them on but she also didn't remember removing her dress. She also didn't find any evidence or get the sense that anyone had touched her against her will. She rolled up her sleeves and discovered that her arms were still stained with her last victim's blood. She frowned and crinkled her nose, suddenly overcome with a desperate need to get clean. Not far from the wardrobe was a door that she hoped would lead to a bathroom with a nice shower. She quickly hopped out of bed to find out.

When Cali opened the door that had caught her eye, she was pleasantly surprised to find a beautiful bathroom with an antique, clawed-foot bathtub. Everything was spotless and neat. On the sink, she found scented body washes and shampoos. There were clean towels, wash cloths organized neatly on racks and a pristine white bathrobe hung neatly on a hook on the back of the door. She strolled over to the tub, turned on the water to run a hot bath and then quickly stripped out of her borrowed pajamas. After carefully weighing her options, she finally decided on a lavender-scented body wash and then slipped into the tub of steaming hot water.

The bath was so relaxing that Cali dozed in and out of sleep as she soaked in the warm water and lost track of time. She felt recharged, invigorated and re-energized. She also started to wonder why she wasn't more suspicious or curious than she was to actually know where she was and what was really going on. After she had killed the last person on her *list*, she had felt lost, like a piece of driftwood from a sunken ship floating in the middle of an ocean. After she had quenched her thirst for revenge, she completely lost her footing but the trio of men that had introduced themselves became a new direction on her inner compass to follow. Still, Cali found it strange that in all the hours that had passed since she woke up, none of her new acquaintances had come to check on her.

"You're finally awake. The way you were sleeping, you must've really been tired," a woman's voice said and when Cali turned her head, she was surprised to see a woman sitting with her legs crossed on the toilet with the lid closed.

The mysterious woman was dressed casually in a plain, white V-neck T-shirt and faded, denim blue jeans with rips in the knees. Her clothes were simple enough but still, everything from the bottoms of her pretty feet to the top of her full head of flaming red hair screamed royalty. They hints of her true station were subtle but her grace and body language screamed that she was a queen of some sort. Cali wasn't sure how she knew, but something deep inside her told her that this woman was much more than what she seemed. The curve of the woman's smile as friendly and welcoming but there was also a stern, unforgiving, unbending strength behind her emerald-green eyes. There was also a long, thin scar across the woman's throat that kept drawing Cali's gaze.

"Who are you?" Cali asked the strange woman.

"Who I am is… complicated," the pale, stunning redhead answered.

"That's the second time in less than twenty-four hours that I've heard that same answer after I've asked that same question," Cali told her.

"For now, you can call me Helga Belegost. That's what the three men that brought you here call me," the woman answered.

"And where are they? The last thing I remember is leaving the nightclub with them. After that, everything is fuzzy, like I dreamed it all," Cali inquired, curious about why half of her night seemed to be missing from her memory.

"They're here. I just thought you'd be more comfortable if I came in to check on you. I'm sure you wouldn't want any strange men hovering over you and interrupting your bath," Helga explained as she stood up.

"And where is *here* exactly?" Cali asked.

"You're in my house," Helga answered vaguely which Cali sensed was intentional and deliberate. "I've laid out some clothes for you in the bedroom. They should fit you much better than Herman's pajamas did," Helga told Cali as she strolled out of the bathroom.

As soon as Helga was gone, Cali sprung up out of the warm bath that had been so soothing and quickly wrapped herself in one of the pristine, fluffy white towels from the towel rack. She felt sober for the first time since she had arrived at Helga's house and her mind was full of questions. Cali wasn't confident that Yusef, Silvio or Herman had the answers that she wanted but, something told her that Helga would.

Back in the bedroom, spread out neatly on the bed were clothes for Cali, just as her mysterious hostess said there would be. The white blouse and the brown leather pants appeared to be a size too small for Cali's thick curves but she was sure that she could wiggle into them. She sighed, glad that she hadn't eaten yet. Otherwise, all of the twisting, stretching and jumping she had to do to force all of her voluptuous body into the clothes might not have worked. The buttons on the blouse barely held together and she had to inhale deeply to fit into the pants but, eventually she managed to squeeze her ass and hips in. She pulled her hair up into a loose bun once she was finally dressed and opened the bedroom door. As soon as she stepped out into the hallway, she found Helga waiting for her

# PART 14

# THE QUEEN'S CASTLE

"You're not afraid. You find yourself delivered to a strange house by very strange people and yet, I don't sense any fear in you. You truly are a beautiful creature," said Helga as she smiled at Cali.

"When you've already died once, there really isn't much more to fear anymore," Cali answered.

Then, Helga stepped so close to Cali that their lips almost touched.

"I knew there was something different, something special about you. Most of you run around doing meaningless things to squeeze as much as you can out of your beautifully short lives as the fear of death...the horror of being cut down by the scythe of the inevitable...drives most of you mad like wild, frightened, stampeding horses. But, here you are," said Helga as she gently touched Cali's cheek. "Unafraid. Fierce. That is so amazing and rare but, ignorance is bliss and there are things much worse than death my dear," Helga told her.

"And what could be worse?" Cali asked, genuinely intrigued. It also did not escape her notice how Helga referred to her as if they were somehow drastically different from each other, as if they weren't just two women having a casual conversation in a hallway of a house. Cali knew what SHE was. She just wondered if Helga was *something else.*

"If you are willing to become what I'm willing to mold you into, you just might find out," Helga answered.

"And what exactly do you plan to try to mold me into?" Cali asked.

"Come," said Helga as she took Cali's hand. "Let me show you around my house."

For the first time since Cali woke up in Helga's house, she felt uncomfortable and uneasy. The way her host had dismissed her question about her true motives made her suspicious although, she did realize that EVERYTHING before that should have made her suspicious as well. She sensed that she had become part of a game on a grand scale that she had never played. Despite not knowing the rules, Cali decided to participate anyway. She relaxed and allowed Helga to lead her through the house.

The hallways were narrow and the walls were so close that there wasn't much room if Cali and Helga walked side-by-side. Cali began to wonder if they were in a mansion because the halls seemed to stretch on and on forever. The strange woman's house did not feel homely, despite how cozy it appeared aesthetically. The vibe inside was more like that of a hotel, as if many souls had passed through there. Deep in the bones of Helga's home, there was an unnatural restlessness. Even time was weird there. No clocks could be found mounted on any of the walls but the minutes that passed by felt like days. Even the sunlight that poured into the house from the large, curtain-less windows seemed strange and unnatural somehow. It wasn't warm on Cali's skin like rays from the sun should be. The glow that penetrated the windows of Helga's house was cold, like the illumination from the fluorescent overhead bulbs that brightened hospital hallways. It made the entire place feel like a clinical, sterile environment and not very homely at all.

During the entire tour, Cali listened to Helga's voice but it was garbled and blurred, as if Cali heard the words from the bottom of a swimming pool. There was something about Helga's house that made Cali feel as disoriented as she had been during her unexpected escape from the nightclub with Yusef, Herman and Silvio. She felt like she was drowning while trapped in the flooded bowels of an old, rusted, sunken ship at the bottom of a cold sea. Somehow, Helga's hand on hers kept her anchored and purposely prevented her from escaping to the surface.

"Good day ladies," a smooth, melodic, male voice greeted them. Silvio flashed his charming grin, full of perfect teeth and then addressed Cali. "It's good to see that you're finally awake. You must have really been tired. You were knocked out for a while," he said as he stood stark naked as the day he was born, dripping wet from head to toe, obviously fresh out of the shower.

Cali gasped and caught her breath like a diver who had just broken the surface of the ocean after a long swim, but not because of Silvio's nude body, despite how chiseled and well-made he was. She felt air rush into her lungs and caught her breath because Helga had finally let go of her hand.

"We have a houseguest. Cover yourself," Helga told Silvio sternly with a hard stare that would have chilled most normal men's blood and sent them scurrying off like a kicked puppy.

"Oh please. I don't have anything that she hasn't seen before," Silvio answered flippantly at first but the curve of his smile straightened when he saw Helga's hand ball up into a tight fist. When he heard her knuckles crack, he knew that she was in no mood for his brash foolishness. "Excuse me ladies. I beg your pardon. I'm off to my room to find some clothes. I apologize and I hope I haven't offended you too much," said Silvio as he bowed his head politely in reverence to them and then took his leave.

"I apologize for that," said Helga to Cali as they both stared at his tight butt cheeks as Silvio strolled away merrily on his way to his bedroom. "That one is like a child with a new toy, I swear. His narcissism is charming at times but Silvio can be too much."

"Do they all live here in the house with you?" Cali asked.

"Yes, and no. They spend time here. They all have their own rooms here and are always welcome here anytime but, they're more like frequent houseguests," Helga answered.

Cali nodded as if that explanation made sense to her and then continued to stroll along at Helga's side, careful not to let Helga take a hold of her hand again.

She kept her arms folded to make sure of that. Something about Helga's touch frightened which was definitely alarming because she did not scare easily.

Cali couldn't clearly describe the house's decor at all. As Helga continued the grand tour, Cali realized that pieces of furniture from many different eras were scattered throughout the home. A professional interior decorator would have had a hard time explaining how all of it, modern furniture mixed up with aging antiques, all seemed to fit together harmoniously. It was as if the past, present and even the future coexisted seamlessly within those walls in such a way that Helga's home felt magical somehow.

"Are you hungry?" Helga asked Cali. "Silly question. Of course you are," Helga continued before Cali even had a chance to answer. "Let's get you something to eat."

## PART 15
# SALT & BREAD

When Cali entered the dining room with Helga, she was surprised to find that two seats at the dining table were already occupied by two women who were completely and deeply engrossed in a heated conversation. Their voices weren't raised but they were clearly having a heated debate, the subject of which Cali couldn't make out because their voices were only slightly louder than whispers as they hissed at each other.

The brunette Latina with the pixie-cut and the piercings in her cheeks was the first to notice that Cali and Helga had walked into the room. For a split second, when their eyes met, Cali could have sworn that the woman's eyes were red…but not bloodshot like someone who needed sleep. She thought that the woman's pupils glowed blood-red before they faded to a hazel brown.

"Is this her?" the tan, honey-colored woman with the piercings and the pixie-cut asked Helga.

"Yes, Veronica. This is Cali," Helga answered.

"You know what she meant!" the other woman at the table added and pounded her meaty fist on the table. She didn't turn her head to look at Cali or Helga. Her skin was as milky and pale as a pristine white bedsheet. Her long locks of blonde hair concealed her face. She was a sturdy, heavyset woman but still curvy, even with all of the extra meat on her bones. Tattoos of skulls, guns, swords, fearsome sea creatures and other grim images that Cali couldn't make out clearly from where she stood covered the exposed parts of the big woman's skin. Cali imagined that underneath her dress, there were many, many more, etched across even more private places.

"Now is not the time, Belladonna," Helga answered her as she balled up her fist and cracked her knuckles again, the same way she had when Silvio had annoyed her a few minutes before.

"Fine," Belladonna answered as she brushed her hair out of her face with her fingers and turned to get a good look at Helga's houseguest.

Without her hair covering her face, Cali saw that Belladonna was very pretty, with plump, rosy cheeks and pouty, pink lips. Her eyes were a little scary and Cali couldn't tell if they were the blue of a clear summer sky or if they were the same shade as the clean waters that surrounded some exotic, untouched tropical island. The way Belladonna's brows were furrowed showed that behind those eyes, there lurked a fury that she kept at bay. She attempted to smile at Cali but the gesture was so forced that it was almost comical. Cali smiled back.

Helga sat down at the head of the long table and motioned for Cali to take the seat to her right. As Cali pulled out the chair and took the place at the table she had been offered, she heard Veronica groan and saw Belladonna frown. Both women stared at Cali with such intensity that her skin felt warm, as if she was a roast, baking in an oven. She only felt slightly relieved when they looked away from her as Yusef walked into the dining room and took a seat on the opposite end of the table in the farthest chair away from Helga.

"Good afternoon ladies," he greeted them all but none of them replied. Cali was the only one to give him a quick little subtle wave to acknowledge him.

For a few minutes after Yusef arrived, no one spoke but the silence wasn't awkward at all and Cali got the sense that these people were used to being together in the same room without speaking. A part of her was also nervous about what would be said, especially about her, once everyone present eventually decided to converse. Helga had been very polite and sweet to her since she introduced herself in the bathroom earlier. The way Yusef smiled at her whenever their eyes met made Cali feel welcome but, the heated discussion combined with the venomous glances in her direction from Belladonna and Veronica did not.

Just as Cali began to wonder how the other two men that she had met with Yusef might tip the scales, for or against her presence, Silvio strolled into the dining room, barefoot but otherwise fully dressed this time in a pink, button-up shirt and a pair of tight blue jeans with rips in the thighs. His hair was tied neatly in a ponytail that ran down his back and nearly stopped at his waist. As he took a seat on Yusef's left side, Cali couldn't help but think of him as a peacock because of the way he seemed to always preen and prance about. However, just underneath the surface of all his fancy, deliberate, metrosexual vanity, she could sense something rotten, almost like a form of decay that would slay anyone, or anything that got too close to him.

"Good afternoon everyone," said Silvio and as he slicked back his hair to make sure that his ponytail was neat with every lock of hair in place, Cali could have sworn that he winked at her.

"Nice shirt pretty boy. That's a gorgeous shade of pink," said Belladonna before she blew Silvio a kiss with her juicy, luscious lips.

"Keep flirting with me like that and you're going to find me knocking on your bedroom door later on tonight, in the wee hours, when I know you have nothing but your pillow between those thick, sexy, chunky thighs. I can just imagine how warm and cozy you are down there," Silvio replied and then smiled with the type of grin that hinted at all the dirty thoughts that ran through his mind as he graphically visualized what he'd do to her.

Belladonna leaned forward and stretched across the table to pinch Silvio's cheek.

"Baby, you wouldn't survive a night between these thighs," she warned him playfully.

"You'd be surprised. I've chopped down bigger trees than you. In another life, I specialized in satisfying big, beautiful women like yourself," he told her.

"In another life, I had a husband who did too. In fact, he satisfied almost every big, beautiful woman for miles around in our town. You remind me of him...your confidence, your swagger, your cockiness," she said and then licked her lips. "In the end. I think I hacked him to pieces with a meat cleaver and then fed him to our hogs," Belladonna confessed while patting Silvio on the cheek before she pulled her hand away and leaned back in her chair with a smug grin.

Silvio was forming his thin, pretty boy lips to say something slick when Herman lumbered into the room and derailed his train of thought.

"Hello everyone. I'm sorry I took so long but, some things, you just can't rush and baking a good loaf of bread is one of them," said Herman as he walked out of the kitchen with a piping hot, fresh load, right out of the oven. He set it down in the middle of the table and was about to start slicing it up when Helga shot him a stern, icy glare that seemed to drop the temperature of the room at least twenty or thirty degrees. "Oh, how stupid of me. How could I forget?" he said and smacked himself on the forehead before he goofily shuffled back to the kitchen like a clumsy, overweight butler. When he returned, he carried a large, round wooden bowl with ornate runes carved into it, filled to the brim and almost overflowing with salt.

Helga looked pleased and Herman looked relieved as he began to slice the hot, sweet-smelling bread. No one at the table uttered a word as Herman skillfully cut perfectly even slices of it for everyone at the gathering and handed them out. Cali thought it was strange that there were no plates or silverware on the table but suddenly, she felt as if she was starving. In fact, as soon as Herman gave her the bread, she could think of nothing else but ravenously devouring it. It took all of the self-control she could muster to not gobble it down before anyone else at the table had taken a bite. Somehow, her instincts and intuition told her that it would have been blasphemous to do so.

After everyone had been given a slice from the loaf, (Herman took two slices for himself but no one seemed to care.) they each extended their hands, palms up, to receive the sprinkle of salt that Herman pinched out of the ornate wooden bowl and gave to them.

"Salt…and bread," said Helga.

"Bread and salt," everyone else at the table, except for Cali, replied in unison.

Cali figured it was their custom. She observed, and then followed their actions when they each put salt on their tongues, then took healthy bites of the bread.

"Now we are bound in friendship, and as family," said Helga as she gently touched Cali on the arm.

"At least, for TODAY we are," Veronica added sarcastically with a sneer. Helga pretended not to hear her.

"Let me introduce you to my other *houseguests*," Helga said to Cali but made sure to emphasize the word "houseguests" as she stared at Veronica before she continued. "Herman, Silvio and Yusef you've already met. The blonde with the tattoos is Belladonna. I would tell you that she's not as mean and surly as she looks or that she's an amazingly sweet cutie-pie inside but, that would be a lie."

"Don't listen to her. I'm really nice…when I want to be…and I'm sweet to people I want to be sweet to," Belladonna chimed in and once again flashed a forced grin in Cali's direction. Then, she kicked Silvio under the table when she felt his toes touch her thigh after he had snuck his foot up her dress.

"The hot tamale with the pixie-cut, cute piercings in her cheeks and the pink streaks in her hair is Veronica…and SHE doesn't have a nice bone in her body," said Helga.

"Don't call me that. It's racist," grumbled Veronica before she ran off a string of curses in Spanish under her breath.

"I apologize. You know that you are my fiery Valkyrie…my STRIFE ," said Helga with deep sincerity in hopes that Veronica's mood wouldn't become even more sour than it already was. At the moment, Helga needed things to go as smoothly as possible.

An oven timer pinged in the kitchen and Herman jumped up from his seat to go see about whatever was ready to be served. Veronica also slid her chair back and got up from the table.

"I'll go and give him a hand," Veronica mumbled.

"Thank you sweetheart," Helga called out to her but Veronica didn't answer or acknowledge her on her way out of the dining room.

The sounds of banging pots and pans proceeded an aromatically amazing assault of unparalleled deliciousness that wafted into the dining room from the kitchen. Cali greedily finished her slice of bread but her tummy still grumbled and she was still starving. She was relieved when Veronica came back with silverware and plates for everyone.

The brunch that Herman had prepared was exquisite. Cali couldn't even name some of the dishes but she was certain that the flavor of everything that touched her lips was some of the best food she had ever tasted. And then there was the wine; an amazing red that quickly mellowed everyone's mood and made them all quite tipsy. Everything that happened after was a blur in Cali's mind. She couldn't hold onto any parts of the conversation but she was certain that there was a cheerful comradery between them all.

After everyone had eaten until they were full and drank the tasty wine until they were drunk, Helga took Cali's hand and walked her out of the dining room. Despite being in a drunken haze, Cali realized that everyone watched them in silence as they left.

"Where are we going?" Cali slurred once she and Helga were back out in the hallway again.

"To my bedroom," Helga answered. "I have something to show you."

# PART 16
# FROZEN IN PHOTOGRAPHS

Helga's bedroom was definitely the largest and most luxurious of all the rooms in the house. It was even larger than any of the common rooms. To call it a *Master Bedroom* would have been an understatement and everything in it, from the ridiculously large bed to the beautiful custom furniture was definitely fit for a queen. The elegance of the room slightly sobered Cali and as she took it all in, Helga casually sauntered across the immaculate, polished, hardwood floor on her way to the bed. Helga let out a weary sigh as she sat down on the edge of the mattress and then kicked off her brown, leather sandals.

"You have questions," Helga said when she noticed that Cali's eyes had settled on the framed photographs and painted portraits that adorned the bedroom walls.

"Who are you people?" Cali asked, in awe of the pictures that seemed alive. Her mind had to fight to remain convinced that they were just still images in beautiful frames, cold and lifeless. The ones that caught her attention were the ones of the people she had just drank wine and shared a meal with. All of their photos seemed fairly recent except for one which looked as if it belonged displayed in the great hall of a museum. Belladonna's picture was actually a painting, faded from age and set in a beautiful, golden frame. The tattooed blonde with the beautifully intense blue eyes was dressed like a pirate with a curved sword on her hip on the deck of a ship with black sails. The artist had even perfectly captured the subtle cuteness of her pretty pink lips and forced smile.

"I'm going to share a part of my story with you because you deserve to hear it. But, I have one condition," said Helga.

"And what condition is that?" Cali asked and folded her arms. She was tired of waiting for straight answers and she didn't like having to bargain or make deals to get them.

"I'm going to share some things with you that are going to sound completely impossible and possibly make me sound like a crazy person. I'm asking you to trust me and know that everything…and I mean *everything* I am about to tell you is the truth. If you promise to have an open mind and believe what I'm about to tell you, then I'll share some things that will answer your questions," said Helga.

"Okay," Cali agreed with sincerity in her eyes but also skepticism in her heart.

"Good. That's good," Helga said and smiled, relieved that Cali seemed willing to open her ears and listen. "Well, by now, I'm sure that you've felt things here aren't exactly what they seem. You might even have sensed that there's something different about this place and the people under my roof…and probably sensed something strange about me too," Helga began.

"Yes, I've felt that," Cali answered, her eyes still drawn towards and fixed on the pictures on the walls.

"None of us are really…how can I say it? *Normal*. The stories of how we all came to be what we are now is quite different for each of us. I'm sure that the others will share their personal stories with you eventually…when they're ready. It's not my place to share their journeys, or their histories but, I will tell you a little bit of mine," said Helga. Then, she took a deep breath like a person who was about to dive into deep waters before she continued. "My story is long, and I don't have the energy or the time to start at the beginning but, I'll start from a point that will help me to answer some of your big questions."

"Fair enough…for now," said Cali.

"Good…that's good," said Helga. Then, she slowly used her pointer finger to trace the line of the thin scar across her neck. "I'm sure you've noticed this, right?" she asked.

"Yes, I noticed it," Cali answered. "How did you get it?" she asked.

Without saying a word, Helga calmly reached over and opened one of the drawers on the nightstand closest to her. She reached into it and took out a knife with a beautiful silver handle. The blade looked sharp enough to slice through anything and Helga held it up in the light to show Cali just how very sharp it was. Cali gasped in horror when Helga smiled at her and then slashed her own wrist with it.

First, frozen in horror, Cali watched as blood gushed from the surgically precise, gruesome wound and dripped down onto the pristine hardwood floor.

Then, she was shocked when the blood suddenly stopped flowing and Helga's wound begin to heal on its own. Her jaw nearly hit the ground when Helga wiped away the blood and the flesh on her wrist was how it had always been, smooth, soft, pink and without even the slightest hint of a scar.

"Now, you're wondering what kind of magic trick or illusion you've just seen...yes?" Helga asked.

"Yes," Cali stuttered, still shocked and confused by what she had just seen.

"It was no illusion. It was no magic trick although, I suppose it's fair to say that some sort of magic just took place. I am not a regular person, in case you hadn't already guessed that and I needed to show you how *not regular* I actually am," Helga began to explain.

Cali's head started to spin as her thoughts became a tornado of confusion, curiosity and complete fascination.

"I don't understand. If your wrist healed like that, how come?" Cali started to ask.

"You want to know how come I have this gruesomely permanent mark on my neck if I'm able to heal the way I just did?" Helga finished Cali's sentence for her. "Well, the reason this cut on my neck never fully healed and left his beautiful scar is because the man who tried to slit my throat used a very dirty trick...something he learned from someone who wanted me dead and shouldn't have shared certain...secrets. You see, that someone who wanted me dead made him coat the blade of his knife with something that she knew would hurt me....a kind of poison that only she knows about. That's why the man who slit my throat nearly killed me. If he had known better, I'm sure he would have taken my head off of my shoulders but instead, he assumed that I would just bleed out so he foolishly left me for dead…a mistake I'm sure he regrets because I keep trying to return the favor," Helga chuckled coldly.

"Does it…hurt?" Cali asked. She had more questions about the people who were trying to kill Helga and why they wanted her dead but for the moment, her brain was busy trying to make sense out of what she had just seen.

"Not anymore," Helga answered as she traced her finger across the thin scar she wore like a choker necklace. "It used to hurt a lot. Now, I'm used to it. I wear it like a tattoo. Belladonna says it gives me character…makes me look more fierce."

"Why would someone try to kill you?" Cali asked.

"A man who wanted information that I didn't want to share decided that he would kill me because I wouldn't help him. The one who sent him to pry secrets from me knew what would happen, knew that I wouldn't help him, knew how things would play out but…that wicked bitch sent him anyway, hoping that he would end my life. He didn't. And now, I'm going to make sure that I end them…both of them," Helga told Cali with callous hate and grim certainty in her voice.

"Why are you telling me this? And what does this have to do with me?" Cali asked, somewhat worried about what Helga's answer might be but also relieved that finally, she was on the brink of hearing the truth about why she had been brought to Helga's strange home.

"That's easy. I want you to help me make them pay," Helga answered, her voice as sweet as honey but anger more bitter than vinegar hidden within her sweetness.

"And why would I want to do that?" Cali asked.

"Because you and I are the same," Helga answered.

"No, we're not," Cali protested.

"Of course we are. You just don't see it. You don't understand what you are," Helga insisted.

"If someone were to cut my wrists, the way you just cut your wrist, I wouldn't heal up like some superhero. I would bleed out and die," said Cali.

"Are you sure? How do you know? Do you really think you're that easy to kill?" Helga asked.

"I'm just a regular person...who has done some very nasty things to people who deserved it. I'm not like you people, whatever you people are," Cali told her.

"I've been watching you. Those men that hurt you tried to kill you...but you didn't die. Why do you think that is?" Helga asked.

"I got lucky. They were sloppy because they panicked, terrified of getting caught and punished for what they had done to me," Cali answered.

"There is no such thing as *luck* in this world, unless it's bad luck. You survived because they *couldn't* kill you. Yes, they wanted you dead to conceal their heinous deed but, they couldn't end your life because you are ⅅEATH," Helga told her.

"What the fuck are you talking about?" Cali asked, even more confused than when Helga had first started talking. "I'm just a woman caught up in some strange shit I really don't understand," she continued and held her head as she felt a serious migraine coming on.

"I have watched you from the moment you were supposed to die in your other life and baby, let me tell you, you are a beautiful creature. I watched you plan, plot and patiently make all of those people that hurt you pay for what they did. No my love, you are not just a *regular* woman but I can only tell someone how beautiful, unique and powerful they are in so many words and in so many ways. In the end, for them to reach their full potential…to unleash their truest nature, they have to believe it…believe in themselves as much as I believe in them. All you have to do is reach out and embrace what you already are," Helga said.

"And how do I do that?" Cali asked, eager to not only make sense of the new life she had chosen but, also to feel like she belonged somewhere. For a long time, she had felt like a ghost trapped among the living. Helga made her feel as if she could learn to be even more than she had been so very long ago, when she had actually felt alive.

"Let me show you," Helga answered as she stood up and extended her hand. "Let me show you."

"And what will it cost me?" Cali asked. She was no fool and already knew that Helga's offer wasn't completely altruistic. There was always a price to pay for everything. That much she had learned in the most painful of ways at the very end of her first life.

"I just want you to be you…who you are…unapologetically powerful and without remorse for being true to your new self," Helga said but, she saw the skepticism in Cali's eager but still slightly hesitant expression. "And of course, I want you to help me get my revenge against those who tried to destroy me…just like you got yours against your enemies. I need you," she added.

"Why me?" Cali asked and as she took Helga's hand in her own, she somehow knew that she had already sealed their deal.

"Because we are kin. We are sisters. We both have a purpose to fulfill. You are the living embodiment of DEATH… its latest reincarnation. I am the living, breathing, embodiment of the CATACLYSM that all earthly cultures speak of and fear. I will feed you…and make you stronger than you ever imagined. They will fear you and no one will ever hurt you again. I am going to set you free to be the immortal that you are," Helga promised and then warmly wrapped Cali tightly in her arms in a loving embrace.

# PART 17

# TRUTH DRENCHED IN DECEIT

For many, many hours that felt like years, Helga shared secrets and histories that were fantastic as well as fearsome. She told Cali about powerful forces that influenced the events that took place on the surface of the spinning Earth. She spoke of things that occurred behind the scenes, well beyond where regular folk were able to see. She told her how it came to be that some beings existed for hundreds, sometimes thousands of years without dying. She explained how all things must end and how everything, even so-called *immortals* could die, if you knew how to kill them. Cali listened to it all and learned how belief and people's faith fueled some, while others continued to survive solely because they did everything in their power to remain hidden. Cali learned the names of beings that no other person had ever heard of and she learned about the true nature of those whose names were familiar to her. Cali also learned about the true nature of her temporary roommates, War…Famine…Pestilence…Strife and Fury. She also learned about herself as Helga tutored her.

The consistent, persistent hooting of an owl somewhere out in the darkness of the night interrupted Helga's lengthy lecture and made both women aware of time again. Cali felt as if she had just woken up from a long nap but she didn't feel rested. Deep in her bones and also in her soul she was weary, exhausted from trying to store and retain all that she had learned which turned out to be a great strain on her brain.

"How long were we talking?" Cali yawned as she rubbed her tired eyes like a sleepy child.

"A very long time," Helga answered. "You're a very good listener and a bright student. You should get some rest. It's late. We can continue, after you've slept."

Cali didn't protest as Helga walked her to the bedroom door. She was eager to get back to her guest room and the unfamiliar, but extremely comfortable bed.

"Yes, I need to sleep," Cali agreed.

"Just keep going down the hall. Your room is the black door with the gold doorknob," Helga directed Cali as she ushered her out into the hallway.

"Thank you," Cali answered, so sleepy and tired that she didn't even notice Yusef who stood in the hall, shirtless and covered in battle scars, leaning against the wall across from Helga's bedroom with his arms folded.

"What do you want?" Helga asked Yusef once Cali was on her way and well out of earshot.

"Let's talk inside," Yusef answered and strolled past Helga into the bedroom. Helga followed.

"What is it? What's the problem now?" Helga asked after she had shut the door behind them.

"Why did you lie to her?" Yusef asked.

"I didn't lie to her," Helga answered, annoyed. She balled both of her hands into fists, a gesture that seemed to frighten all of the others but Yusef was unmoved.

"You did," he insisted as he stared down at Helga who was much shorter than he was.

"I did not!" Helga bellowed angrily as she stared up into his dark, burning eyes beneath his troubled, furrowed brow. The way he towered over her made her uncomfortable she didn't appreciate it at all.

"Before she ever came to this house, before I brought her here because you asked me to, she was already everything that you just convinced her that you made her," he said.

"Yes, of course she was…but she didn't know that," Helga answered. "And if I didn't show her what she was, she would've lived out her days as a mortal, and died as one when her time came simply because she wouldn't have known that she didn't have to die so young…never would have known that she could've kept on living for hundreds, maybe thousands of years. What I gave her was a gift. I gave her the truth, even if I made it seem like her power came from me. So what? That's better than the alternative, isn't it? To fade away in the blink of an eye…especially after such a brief, painful, tragic life as the one she had lived, full of brutality and pain."

"What you gave her…was a lie. You made her feel as if she owes you for a gift that was never yours to give because it was already hers. Now, she feels obligated to be on your side and to do your bidding," said Yusef.

"There is ONLY my side! Who else would FAMINE PESTILENCE STRIFE FURY DECEIT WAR & DEATH herself serve if not me?" Helga asked and the foundation beneath the house shook violently as she named them all.

"Who knows? Maybe someone better," Yusef answered as he turned his back on Helga on his way to the bedroom door.

"Be careful. Some conflicts are impossible to win. Some enemies are too strong to overcome," she warned and threatened him as he walked away.

"Of course. But, I wage war for the sake of it. Conflict, no matter who wins, or who loses, feeds me and gives me power," he answered as he left her room.

Helga grunted and slammed her bedroom door behind him. She sensed that a storm was brewing between herself and WAR and she was not pleased.

When Cali was in Helga's room, if she had known to look, or paid close enough attention, she would've noticed a very odd photograph on the wall amongst the others that had caught her attention. In that photo was the blurred image of a very thin man who was almost as tall as Yusef, dressed in a gray suit, the color of winter storm clouds. The face beneath the top hat the man in the photo wore was blurred

103

despite the rest of the photo being sharply in focus. Almost as soon as Helga's bedroom door was shut, that man from that painting stepped out of the shadows in the far corner of the room to greet her with a courteous bow and a broad, shark-like smile. His skin was an odd, light shade of gray that made it almost impossible to see him outside of the light. He was like a living shadow cast on concrete.

"It's my nature to lie, and to deceive but, just this once, I'll share a hard truth with you," whispered the thin man.

"And what's that, Lucius?" Helga asked as she walked over to the elegant cabinet where she kept almost every type of alcohol and stimulant ever created throughout the long history of the world.

With an almost clumsy, jittery stride, DECEIT walked over to the red, leather chair in front of the wall where his own blurred photograph hung, sat his lanky body down and crossed his long legs. He looked almost like a spider as he clasped his hands.

"That one," he said with disdain, as if the words tasted bad in his mouth, "Yusef...your WAR has a thing for your newly anointed goddess of DEATH. Be careful my mistress, my omnipotent and wise queen. He will betray you if he has to choose between you," Lucius warned Helga.

"I know," she answered as she started to pour herself a tiny glass of absinthe almost the same shade of green as a pit viper.

## EPILOGUE

# THE TOWER OF SEVEN

After much training, and studying, and learning, Cali finally set out to murder the man who had slit Helga's throat. His name was Seven and Cali had been climbing the stairs of his dark, towering skyscraper for what seemed like forever. Helga had warned her that she would feel unnaturally weary and be tempted to turn back. She also told Cali to keep walking up the stairs, no matter what because the elevators were booby-trapped. After almost two years of rigorous, vigorous, intense training, Cali did not want to disappoint her sister who had invested so much time and energy in her so, on and up she continued to march, higher and higher, level after level.

Just before her spirit broke, she finally reached the final floor at the very top of the skyscraper. She left the last stairwell through a heavy, metal door below a glowing red exit sign.

The air was cold in the hallway that led to the doors that guarded Seven's penthouse suite. It was deathly, eerily quiet and she might have been afraid if she had not been given a great gift from her immortal mentor, a weapon of legend that she had heard of in fairytales even before Helga shared the true tale of its creation. Cali felt brave as she gripped the handle of the sword that had once been stuck in an ancient, moss-covered stone until the hand of a king removed it and set it free. The well-balanced weight of the steel gave her strength and settled her nerves as she approached the shiny ebony doors that stood between her and her prey. She took one last deep breath before she kicked the doors wide open.

On the other side of the doors, Cali found herself standing in an enormous office with windows that stretched from the floor to the ceiling. There was very little furniture but the dark desk and the throne-like black chair on the opposite side of the room gave it the appearance of the office of an important CEO. Cali felt a slight electrical charge spark through her body. The room looked modern but the vibe inside resonated with the unmistakable pulse and energy of a holy place...not unlike a temple where people came to worship. The smooth, black tiles that covered the floor were like mirrors and as she slowly strolled across them, Cali felt as if she was walking across a dark, frozen lake. She looked down at her own fearsome reflection and when she looked up again, she saw him. Seven stood in front of one of the large windows behind his desk, sipping clear rum from a shot glass with his back to her as he peered out at the torrential rain that poured down on the city. The lights in the room were dim so only when the lightning from the storm flashed did she get a clear look at him, in his black suit, with his dark skin, sullen and grim. His reflection in the window showed that he was a black man, somewhat handsome with a neatly-trimmed, close-cropped beard.

"The enemy of my enemy was my friend once," said Seven.

Something in his voice made Cali stop walking towards him. There was power in it but, it was not threatening, at least not yet. Then, the same curiosity that had driven her to follow Yusef, Silvio and Herman once suddenly compelled her to hear what the one she had been sent to kill had to say.

"I am not your friend," Cali told him dryly.

"Of course you aren't," Seven laughed. "I was talking about a different one, from a different time...one much older and stronger than you. You are just a baby, a new recruit, a green novice and a pawn of the one who sent you, the one whose head I nearly added to my collection," he told Cali and made a slicing motion across his neck that made the image of Helga's scar burn brightly in Cali's mind's eye. "And, the one who sent you is just a pawn of others that are more powerful and much older than she is. The one I speak of, the enemy of my enemies who pretended to be my friend is the enemy of the one who sent you and also the mortal foe of the ones she serves."

"Who and what are you talking about?" Cali asked, annoyed that Seven seemed to be speaking in riddles.

"Once upon a time, the immortal who rules the seas saved my life after I was left for dead by another of her kind, way back when I was just a mortal man," Seven answered.

"Poseidon? Neptune?" Cali asked with a hint of snarky disbelief, despite all of the *impossible* things she had come to believe and in spite of all that Helga had shown her of the hidden truths.

"No. The sea god of the Greeks and the Romans is long gone and in his place rules another…and she is powerful…more powerful than the others before her…and she is angry. She has been poisoned, and tainted, and she is in constant pain. Still, she took pity on me once as I lay bleeding on a beach. She pulled me to her breast when the tide got high and dragged me down to the deep places that sailors fear. Do you want to know what I saw there?" Seven asked.

"What did you see?" Cali asked.

"I saw rusty chains, corroded by the salty waters…chains and shackles on the ocean floor for as far as my eyes could see, down in the dark, at the bottom of her sea. And then, when I couldn't hold my breath any longer and my lungs began to fill with water, I saw the lost souls of those who had been stolen from their continent and cruelly sold into slavery. All of them had skin as dark as mine, some even darker. I saw every man, woman and child who had been tossed overboard the slaver's ships during centuries and centuries of that evil middle passage. They were the lost and the forgotten. As I drowned, the sea goddess who saved me told me their story and I learned that all of those drowned souls were the soldiers of her army. That's when I struck a deal at the bottom of that ocean, where sea monsters lurk, down in the deep, far away from where sunlight can reach. Do you know why I don't die, even though I was born a mortal man?" Seven asked.

"Why?" Cali asked because, when she heard him speak with such surety and confidence, she couldn't help but wonder if Helga's plan, her dirty trick to make his immortal heart stopped ticking would even work.

"I don't die because every time my lights go out and should be out for good, one of those lost ones in her watery, salty court sacrifices their light so that I can burn brightly again. So, much like the old myths about cats, I have many, many lives…even more than I can count…enough to outlast all of those who would see me dead. Now, my question to you is, what do you really hope to accomplish by ending just one of those lives if I'm guaranteed to come back to life? Do you plan to kill me a hundred times? A thousand…over and over again until all of the lights that would spark mine again are used up and extinguished? I'm sure that Helga has taught you some ancient trick that she thinks will work this time but, the last time she tried, I gave her that thin red gift she wears across her throat like a necklace. Do you even know who she really is and what she hopes to bring about?" Seven asked.

"I haven't cared much for the world in a very long time. A CATACLYSM isn't such a bad idea to me. Maybe it should all be destroyed so something better can take its place," she answered.

"Maybe," Seven answered. He wasn't very fond of what the world had become either. With one last gulp, Seven finished the dregs of liquor left in his shot glass. He still didn't turn around to face Cali. Instead, he stared out of the window that overlooked his city. He studied the lights in the other buildings and the buzz of the busy streets below. "I've told you a lot about myself but you haven't told me anything about yourself. For our kind, when we meet for the first time, it's somewhat customary to share something about ourselves before a duel. I usually don't care much about the old rules or proper etiquette but, when it comes to these kinds of things…the killing…I hate to admit that I'm fond of the rituals and traditions. After all, there's a good chance that after tonight, one of us will never get to tell anyone our story again. I mean, someone somewhere will tell our tale, or at least their interpretation of it but, I think it's tragic whenever we don't get to tell our story ourselves, from our own perspective," he said with his back still turned to her.

"I never really liked my story much anyway so it really doesn't matter to me," Cali answered. "Maybe the next person who tells it, IF I die here tonight and someone else HAS to tell it, will make it more interesting than I ever could have," she continued as she tried to regain confidence in Helga's plan and confidence that she could execute it. Seven had done a great job of causing her concern and filling her heart with doubt.

"I suppose I'll have to guess what you are, who you are, since you're not willing to share," said Seven. Then, he put his palm on the cold glass of the window and felt the rhythm of the raindrops as they beat against it. In the vibration and deliberate pattern of the tapping of the splattering rain there was a hidden message that only he could decipher. He heard the voice of the immortal who had saved his life and gifted him with so many more. He smiled as the sea goddess shared secrets with him. "You are not FURY. That chunky blonde pirate would have never made it up all those stairs," he joked cruelly. "And Helga would have never trusted PESTILENCE or FAMINE to come claim my head. She also knew better than to send STRIFE who would've stormed in here recklessly and would already be dead. And, I bet Helga didn't tell you that I've slaughtered the last four incarnations of ᴅWAR that she has sent after me. I love a good, bloody brawl though. But you don't look like a brawler. I wish she had sent him instead of you, I truly do…but I'm sure that she's figured out that no matter what, he won't win. I've got four skulls in my ever-growing collection to prove it. ᴅECEIT is a coward who skulks about in the dark whispering and deplores getting his hands dirty so, you are definitely not that one. So, that leaves only one so I'm assuming that you are Helga's new goddess of ᴅEATH," he said and then turned around to look directly at Cali for the first time since she had kicked opened his doors.

"I thought the skull makeup I painted on my face was a dead giveaway," she joked.

"Did Helga tell you why the others have tasked her with killing me? No? Well, I don't suppose she would willingly share her fuck up with you. You see, she sent another ᴅEATH for me before. After he failed, I didn't kill him though. I didn't end his life. I kept him alive for a long time and forced him to share all of his secrets…all of the tricks he'd learned, a wealth of knowledge about the methods I would need to execute every single one of these so-called *immortals* who have plagued this world for far too long.

"So we both serve destruction, you for your own reasons and me for mine," said Cali as she raised the weapon she had been holding at her side so that he could have a good look at it.

Seven immediately recognized the Arthurian sword that his sea goddess ally, the legendary ᴅLADY OF THE ᴅLAKE herself, had crafted once for a king. Still, he was not afraid. Even if Cali managed to mortally wound him with it, he was certain that he would not remain dead. Because of the suicidal thoughts he constantly wrestled with, he secretly hoped that a weapon created by the power that fueled his immortality might be enough to finally end him. He wouldn't mind the eternal rest at all. His only regret would've been that he hadn't finished what he started with his very personal quest for revenge against those who had wronged him. However, no matter how confident and fierce his opponent appeared to be, deep down he doubted that she could do what she came to do.

"You think Helga sent you here to kill me, don't you? Shit…I'm sure SHE thinks she sent you here to kill me but she's wrong. Do you know why?" Seven asked with an icy grin that sent a frigid chill of uncertainty creeping up Cali's spine. "The truth is, beautiful woman, you won't be able to kill me. The truth is that Helga sent you here to die."

The story continues on the pages of

"Cursed Immortals"

# AFTERWORD

I hope that you've enjoyed this novella which tried its hardest to become a full-length novel against my will and original intentions. An early, abbreviated version of it appeared in "Crossroads 2: An Anthology" but after the anthology was published, I felt in my heart that "Slow Kiss of the Apocalypse" was much too important to let it stand as just a short story. As I began to flesh out the characters, I realized that they were part of a much bigger world that had been living and expanding inside my head. I felt the common thread but didn't clearly see the connection until after the release of my urban thriller, "Death in the City," which was a beast to write and temporarily distracted me from all of the other stories living in my head. It was a relief to be done with it and as soon as I scribbled the last words at the end of its last chapter, another story started to scream at me again. That noisy, complicated, epic tale needed to be told and it wouldn't allow me to ignore it any longer. That's when I started to write scenes for "Cursed Immortals" again. Somehow, I could feel Seven staring down at me from the top floor of his terrible, monstrous skyscraper with his dark piercing eyes.

(Even an immortal's patience has limits.) It also suddenly dawned on me that Cali's world and Seven's were the same. Both character's mortal lives ended in tragedy and both of them were seeking revenge for what had been done to them. Somehow, they just ended up on opposite sides with different allies.

"Slow Kiss of the Apocalypse" is basically the prequel to "Cursed Immortals." I wanted to use this book to tell a very surrealistic and gritty tale that gradually pulled you into a hidden world adjacent to the real one we live in. By the end of the novella, I wanted you to feel that there is much more going on than you may have originally thought as you flipped through the early pages. The epilogue has set the stage for some awesome things to come and I promise that I won't take long to show you what happens next.

-Keith Kareem Williams
May, 15, 2017

# Cursed Immortals

# 1 Godling

"Godling" is what the elders called him, as an insult and as a sign that they did not truly believe that he belonged among them. He represented something new and something for the *fearless* to fear. He sat in his penthouse suite, in his dark throne, at the top of his dark tower and stared out into the brightly lit blackness of the filthy city below. Just above his head, there was an invisible crown that he would have gladly traded for a halo because, that night, he wished that he was dead. *"Seven"* was the name he preferred, although it had not been his name when he had just been a man. It was simple and reminded him that he had once been the same as the people he watched scrambling around below, constantly running from 𝒟EATH. There were other names that he had been branded with against his will, *"The Bastard King," "The Sword of the Faithless," "The Heathen's Scythe,"* and *"The Savage Reaper"* but his favorite was still plain *"Seven"* because it was the number of so-called immortals he had killed to become immortal himself.

# ABOUT THE AUTHOR

**Keith Kareem Williams** is the author of 13 books & currently working on his 14th. He still resides in his hometown of Brooklyn, New York where he delicately balances his time between his responsibilities as a single father as well as the challenges of being a full-time author.

"In interviews, one of the most difficult questions I've been asked is, *'What genre are your novels?'* because honestly, I never write with any particular style in mind. I enjoy blending styles and mashing different genres together in interesting ways. Basically, I pen whatever is in my heart and soul. However, if I had to describe my style I would use musical terms and say that I write Urban, Hip-Hop, fiction with the rhythm of Reggae that crashed into Heavy Metal and then began to bleed Neo Soul. I call it *Alternative Urban Fiction*.©"

One of the things I'm most proud of is how my children look at me with pride because I'm accomplishing my goals and doing the things I set out to do with my career. They recognize and respect my passion. I write constantly and I already have the titles & plots lined up for my next 69 novels. This is what I do and I'm just trying to let the rest of the world know this. My ambition is to become as legendary as some of the writers I admire. I believe that a GOOD writer pulls you into their story. A GREAT writer makes the world around you fall away as you read. The LEGENDARY writers tell stories that become a part of you and linger long after you've read the last line of the last chapter. It was once said that, *the pen is mightier than the sword*. I say to my fellow AUTHORS: Let's advance our craft until it's mightier than guns, grenades, bullets & nuclear bombs. If not, then put your pen down and fall back. Those of us who are serious about this will run you over as if we were riding in tanks."

**Books by Keith Kareem Williams**

Water Flows Under Doors (2004)
Open Spaces (2010)
Sometimes Brooklyn, Mostly Mars (2011)
Crossroads: an Anthology (2011) *co-written with K R Bankston, Elizabeth LaShaun, and Keith Gaston*
Glass Goddesses, Concrete Walls (2012)
War Angel (2013)
War Angel II: Where Angels Fear to Tread (2014)
Tourniquet (2014)
Blood & Vengeance (2014) co-written with *Keith Gaston*
Crossroads 2 (2015) *co-written with K R Bankston, Elizabeth LaShaun, and Keith Gaston*
War Angel III: Catalina (2015)
The Higher Learning Curve (2016)
Sometimes Brooklyn, Mostly Mars Volume 2 (2016)
Death in the City (2016)

If you wish to contact the author, you can reach him via his email address: kkareemwilliams@gmail.com

You can also follow the author online:

Website: www.reemafterdark.wix.com/reemafterdark
Twitter: @reemafterdark
Blog: www.reemafterdark.blogspot.com
Instagram: Reemafterdark
Facebook: Keith Kareem Williams